STALEMATE

MURDOCH MAFIA NOVELLA

SAMANTHA BARRETT

For my uncle Antz,
The baddest motherfucker I have ever known, this one's
for you Uncle, you inspired my inner gangster to write
these mafia books.
Keep it fucking real Uncle, until we meet again.

Chapter One

Kiara

Start before you're ready. Don't prepare, just begin.

THAT IS THE MANTRA I HAVE LIVED MY LIFE BY SINCE I was a teenager. If I didn't, I wouldn't be where I am today or who I am. That motto is the reason I am married to the man I have been in love with my whole life. He is the best thing that ever happened to me. Bish is my better half in every sense of the word. He's over the top protective but at the same time attentive and caring, making me feel loved and cherished daily. He was my sole focus and center of my world until the day I gave birth to our son. Staring down at the framed photo in my hands, the image of my son and his father has tears of thankfulness clouding my vision.

Royal is a picture perfect image of his father except for the eyes, he has my pale blue color. They don't see the likeness they share but I do—from the back, you can't tell them apart. I have tried to discourage Royal from covering his body in ink but I know I am fighting a losing battle. He has always loved the beautiful art that covers his father's entire body and I can't blame him, seeing Bishop shirtless with all his ink on display still takes my breath away and has me becoming a wanton mess for my man.

My phone begins to ring, pulling me from my inner thoughts. Sighing, I place the photo back where it belongs before pulling my phone from my pocket. I smile at the sight of my husband's name flashing across the screen, and I answer without hesitation.

"Hey, handsome."

The sigh that escapes him tells me he's stressed. Lately, he has been under a shitload of pressure and I hate that I can't help him. With the passing of my father, Bishop has had no choice but to step up and take over Miami as well as run New York so no other family can try to encroach on our territory.

"Where are you?" The demand in his voice has me bristling but I bite my tongue, I've learned to pick and choose my battles over the years. He knows better than anyone that I don't take well to someone demanding things from me or trying to tell me what to do.

"In our bedroom, why?"

"I need you in my office, now!" Before I can reply, the bastard ends the call, and my anger peaks. I storm out of our bedroom and stomp my feet the whole way to his office. You know what I said about picking my battles? Well, this is one of those times when I know I'm about to go to war. Bishop Murdoch may be the Don of New York and now Miami but that title doesn't mean shit in our marriage. In this family no one is above the other. We are equal, a team, partners if you will.

I don't stop as I reach his office. I shove the door open, ready to go a round with my husband and show him what ordering me around gets him, but at the sight in front of me, I freeze. Dozens of vases filled with black roses are set up all over the room—the room is covered! I slowly look toward my man, who leans against his desk with his ankles crossed and his arms gripping his desk on either side of him. My greedy eyes drink him in, his black slacks hugging his thick thighs perfectly. The white button-down shirt he wears has the top few buttons undone exposing a sliver of skin, and his sleeves are rolled up to his elbows exposing the ink that covers his hands and forearms. His black hair is now tinged with specks of gray but it enhances his beauty and gives him more of a bad boy edge.

The raw sex appeal rolling off him has me fighting

not to clench my thighs and telling him to fuck me right here, right now just so he can rid me of the ache the sight of him has caused.

"You still mad?" The playful tone of his voice has me remembering why I stormed down, I school my features and try to hold onto my earlier anger as I glare at my husband.

"Yes."

He rolls his full lips over his teeth to keep from smiling. "Do you know what you're mad about?"

Narrowing my eyes I nod. "Yes."

He pushes off his desk and eats up the space between us in five long strides. He doesn't stop until he is flush against me, forcing me to crane my neck to maintain eye contact. It's times like this that I hate the height difference between us. I may be small but you best believe I can hold my own against these Murdoch men and their big dick energy. A gasp escapes me the moment he snakes his arm out and grips the back of my neck forcing me up onto my tiptoes. He stares down at me with an unreadable expression on his face, then bends until his lips ghost over mine.

"Tell me why you're mad?"

A shiver rolls through me. I'll admit, it takes a shit load of effort to keep myself from moaning. I fucking love it when he gets like this and goes alpha male and shit on me, demanding dirty things and showing me without words that we are fucking cosmic.

"Y-you." I stop and clear my throat hating the way his eyes shine with laughter knowing he has me right he where he wants me—wanton and needy to the point I'll cave and let him win this argument just so he'll lay me down on his desk and fuck me until I come so hard I nearly pass out. "You were being a bossy prick."

A dark chuckle escapes him. "Hmmmm." A small moan does escape me when his free hand grabs my ass. I hate that with a simple touch, he is able to make me forget that I was so mad at him. I swear he has magical powers or something because fuck me, this man can piss me off like no other but he is also the only one who can rid me of my anger with a single touch or look. "You love it when I'm bossy though," he whispers against my lips, then places a chaste kiss to the corner of my mouth and runs his nose down the column of my neck. I tilt my head back trying to give him better access but he tightens the grip on my neck and growls.

"Bishop…" I whine. He pulls me up just enough to place open mouthed kisses on the side of my neck then moves so the tips of our noses touch, his brown eyes boring into mine. The lustful look in his gaze has my breath hitching and my thighs clenching.

"What's wrong, baby?"

I humph out my displeasure and try to look pissed off but the light laugh that escapes him tells me I am failing miserably. "You know what's wrong." I can hear how breathy I sound and know without a doubt I have just lost this battle and I can't find it within myself to care. I just need him to rid me of this ache between my legs and have me seeing stars as I come all over his glorious cock.

"But, you're pissed off at me, remember?"

I decide to take the reins and try to control this situation so I can get what I want. I wrap my arms around his neck and lift my leg, locking it as best as I can around his waist. The way his eyes narrow tells me I am getting the upper hand and I fucking love it, there is no feeling more powerful than bringing a man like Bishop Murdoch to his knees.

"You rang and barked orders at me–" my retort is cut off when he shifts his hold, grips the backs of my thighs and lifts me. My legs lock around him and my arms tighten around his neck. A smile spreads across my face as I stare down at the man I could only dream of loving me when I was growing up. The way he looks at me now is how I always wished he would and fuck me, it is an intoxicating feeling knowing I literally got the man I have loved my whole damn life.

"I knew your angry ass would come storming down here ready to fight."

Frowning down at him I ask, "Why not just ask me to come down here like a normal person?"

"Because nothing about us is normal, baby." I swoon.

"Why am I here, Bish?" I know regardless of what he is saying there is a reason he called me down here and why there are dozens of roses littering his office. He moves over to the two-seater couch in here and sits, forcing me to adjust my position so I'm straddling his lap. Reaching up he tugs the elastic from my hair and fluffs it out. He's always loved my long black hair. He smiles up at me but I can see in his eyes something is weighing on him. You can't force Bishop to talk, he is the type of man you just have to wait for him to figure shit out in his head before he can express himself.

"Most people celebrate their anniversaries on the day they made it official and became a couple." Confusion swarms inside me at his words. "Thing is, we aren't most people like I said. For the past twenty years, you have asked me why on the fourteenth of May I buy you roses and take you out somewhere nice or buy you lavish gifts and all that shit. Want to know why?"

I feel like this is a trap but curiosity always gets the better of me. "You know I do."

Reaching up he cups my face and leans forward until our foreheads are touching. "You choose to acknowledge the day we became official as our anniversary but I don't. May fourteenth is the day I choose to celebrate because it's the day you first walked through the front door of this house." My eyes widen and begin to fill with tears. "I knew from the first moment I saw you that you were going to change my life. I had no idea then, given our age gap, that I would fall madly fucking in love with you or that you would become my wife or the mother to my son. May fourteenth is the day I celebrate because you gave me a reason to hope, baby." A lone tear slides down my cheek, he swipes it away with his thumb before placing a soft kiss on my lips.

"I had no idea," I whisper.

He smiles sadly and nods. "I know. Just your presence in this house gave me a reason to fight for more and the courage to get my siblings out from under our father's torment. You had no idea the effect you had on me. I was a fool for letting you run from me, keeping my distance, hoping that you would be able to live a normal life without me."

"Bishop, I was nothing without you. I was just a shell, an empty vessel without any meaning."

"You are everything, Kiara Murdoch," he growls. "You gave me the strength to do what I needed to, so I could save my family. The moment you accepted that scholarship I knew I wouldn't be able to stay away from you. You are my everything. Without you, I am nothing, baby. I swore to you years ago on the day you agreed to love me until death that I would always be here loving you until my last breath. Shit, I'd still love you in the afterlife because you are mine no matter what!"

My heart swells inside my chest.

Unable to form words, I decide to show him how fucking much I love him and feel the exact same way. Without Bishop I am nothing. I love our son with every fiber of my being but Bishop is my soul. The only reason I would go on living in this world without him is because a part of him lives within our son. I mesh my lips to his and groan the moment his tongue invades my mouth, my senses kicking into overdrive at the taste of him.

Our hands are frantically touching each other, even after all these years we can't seem to get enough of each other. I break our kiss, grip the lapels of his shirt and tear it open. Buttons fly everywhere but neither of us gives a shit. My lips are back on his in seconds as my hands roam all over his tattooed torso. He growls into my mouth the moment I grind down on his hardening cock. He grips my sports bra and yanks it over my head, freeing my tits, my nipples hard and begging for attention. Bishop cups them in his hands, flicking his thumbs over my hardened peaks, drawing a strangled moan from me.

"Fuck, I love these tits, baby," he grits out. I throw my head back and cry out the moment he leans forward and sucks on my nipple. Jesus, the moment he swirls his tongue over it I feel myself soak through my panties. The ache in my core builds. I press down against him, needing friction, but he uses his free hand to clamp down on my waist and hold me still. He switches sides and pays my other nipple the same amount of attention. It's fucking driving me crazy.

"Bishop, I need you inside me now," I cry out when he bites down lightly on my nipple. He releases it with a wet pop and stares up at me with a devilish smile.

"Are you fond of these yoga pants?" Frowning, I shake my head unsure of what the hell he means until he reaches between our bodies and tears the crotch of my pants. Before I can say a word or chastise him for tearing my pants he shoves my soaked panties to the side and buries two fingers inside my tight wet pussy, drawing a sharp cry of pleasure from me. He continues to finger fuck my greedy little cunt as he grips the back of my neck with his other hand and yanks me forward until our foreheads touch. "You like that?"

My face contorts in pleasure as he curls his fingers inside me and hits that sweet spot. "Yes," I pant.

"You want to come on my fingers or my cock?"

"Oh, God," I cry out. I can feel my orgasm cresting and try with all my might to latch onto it but the bastard slows his pace. "Bishop!" I scold, his gaze hardens and he stops moving inside me.

"Answer me, now."

"What?" In my foggy brain, I can't remember what the fuck the question was.

"You coming on my fingers or my cock, Princess? Choose now or you don't come and you're gonna suck my dick instead." I gape down at my husband, after all these years he should know by now I don't do well with ultimatums. I press up on my knees and almost whimper when his fingers slip out of me. The moment I stand, he begins to frown. I don't hesitate, gripping his hair and pulling him forward until his face is buried inside my pussy. His hands grip my ass to keep me steady as he pushes his tongue inside me.

"Fuck!" I cry out as a shudder rolls through me from the pleasure he is drawing out of me. God, this man knows how to play my body like a master puppeteer.

Gripping his hair to hold him in place I grind against his face chasing my orgasm but my panties keep getting in the way, as if he can read my mind, he shreds my pants further, tearing my panties from my body. I expect him to throw them to the side but the moment he reaches up and stuffs them in my mouth I groan. I can taste my arousal and fuck if it doesn't cause more moisture to gather at my center. Fuck, I love when he goes all beast on me and causes carnage to my body. Something about that shit is just so hot.

"Ride my fucking face, baby." I do as he commands, grinding down onto his waiting tongue and chasing my release. I reach up and twirl my nipples between my fingers. His grip on my ass tightens as he sucks my clit into his mouth, then without warning my orgasm rips through me.

"Bishop..." I scream as I flop forward gripping the back of the sofa to try to keep myself upright as my orgasm takes over. He continues to lap at my pussy as shudders roll through me. I feel him undoing his pants, causing anticipation to thrum through me, knowing how fucking good it's going to feel having his cock inside me.

"Sit on my fucking cock, princess." I eagerly obey his demand and shift until I'm kneeling on either side of his thick thighs, his massive cock resting against his abs. My mouth waters at the sight of pre-cum on the head. Needing a taste, I swipe my finger over the tip and bring it to my lips. Bish's gaze is laser focused on my mouth. I dart my tongue out and taste him, instantly my eyes slam closed and a whimper tumbles from my lips at the taste of him. My pussy clenches on air as I suck the digit into my mouth. Impatient as always, Bishop grips my hip with one hand and uses his other to guide his cock to my entrance.

Without warning or gentleness he slams inside me, drawing a strangled scream from me, fuck. The feeling of him stretching and filling me to the brink is fucking perfection. He wraps one arm around my waist, then buries the other in my hair, yanking on my strands to tilt my head back as he leans forward and sucks on my neck, marking me. I start to ride him, not able to stay still any longer. Groans tumble from him as he continues to kiss, suck, nip and lick his way down to my tits, where he sucks one of my nipples into his mouth.

I reach out and brace my hands on his shoulders for leverage as I begin to bounce up and down on him. I'm so fucking horny, I can feel myself getting wetter with each thrust. The only sounds that can be heard are our moans and skin slapping against skin. He releases my nipple with a pop before he claims my lips, swallowing my moans. Just like I knew he would, he begins to thrust up inside me, needing to be in control. Bishop has to be in control inside and outside of the bedroom—it's what makes him, *him*. I can't stop it, another orgasm tears through me, I see stars and my vision turns hazy.

One day he is going to kill me from such intense pleasure.

"Fuck, baby, I'm gonna cum," he grits out. I meet him thrust for thrust, needing to feel him fill me up. He comes roaring my name and fuck me if that isn't the hottest sound I have ever heard in my life. It makes me feel fucking powerful, knowing I am the one who can bring him to such a height of pleasure.

We're both breathing erratically. I flop forward and rest my face in the crook of his neck as his arms band around me, holding me close. He places a kiss on the top of my head. I smile up at him as I place a soft kiss on the underside of his jaw.

"I love you, princess." My heart warms hearing those words. I'll never tire of hearing them from him.

"I love you more than you will ever know, Bish."

I could stay here forever basking in the love that can be felt in this room but the moment is ruined when his phone begins to ring. I attempt to hop off his lap but he locks his arm around me, holding me in place as he reaches down and fishes his phone out of the pocket of his slacks. The devilish smile that stretches across his face has me frowning, wondering who the hell it could be to inspire such a look on his face. He answers the call and places it on speaker.

"What can I do for you, son?" My eyes widen and I

try to push against his chest but he pins me with a warning look and refuses to let me go. I narrow my eyes back at him.

There is no way I am going to speak to my son while his father's cum is being held inside me by his cock!

"Why did you tell Uncle Vin he couldn't teach me and Chanel anymore?" Royal sounds pissed off and I sigh. Bishop and Royal love each other but they butt heads all the time. Royal is trying to prove to his father that he is ready to take over as the head of the family but Bishop doesn't want that for him. He wants our son to go experience life before he is tied to this one with no freedom and no escape. Hence why they are always butting heads and fighting, because they are both too fucking stubborn and refuse to tell the other their reasoning.

"Because you both don't need any more training–"

"The hell we don't!" Royal snaps, cutting his father off. The angry glint that enters Bishop's eyes has me tensing, I reach out and place my hand against his chest, trying to calm him but it's futile.

"Listen to me, you little shit–" I tear my hand back and glare down at my husband. He snaps his gaze to mine and his brows raise knowing he just fucked up big time.

"Don't you ever talk to my baby like that!" I snap.

"He isn't a fucking baby!"

"Mom?" Bishop and Royal both say in unison.

"I don't give a shit if he is nearly twenty-one or not,

he will always be my baby!" I snarl at his father before taking the phone from Bishop and speaking to my son. "Yes, I'm here." I gasp and try to scramble out of Bishop's hold. He leans forward and captures my nipple between his teeth.

"Mom, can you tell Dad–"

"Bishop, stop!" I chastise him and continue to try to wiggle free but when I feel his cock hardening inside me, I freeze. The dirty devil releases my nipple and smirks up at me.

"Mom? What's going on?" Before I can answer, Bishop snatches the phone off me and answers our son.

"No more training of any kind for you. Finish school and be a kid while you can."

"But, Dad–"

"No buts, Royal. No more training. I mean it. Now fuck off and go party or something, I'm trying to make you a sister." I gasp and scowl at him but he just laughs.

"Oh that is fucking nasty, you're too old for that shit–" Bishop ends the call and tosses his phone to the side.

"I'll show that prick who is too old to fuck." Laughter bursts out of me when he flips us so I'm on my back and he looms above me. That is how we spend the rest of the afternoon, fucking on every surface of his office and ignoring our son's calls.

I just wish I knew then that this might be the last moment we would share together like this.

Chapter Two

Knight

"WHAT IS IT, NOW?" I BARK THE MOMENT KING walks into my office at the gym. My brother sighs and drops down into the chair in front of my desk. He looks tired and wrung out. That's what this life does to you, it ages you and forces you to look over your shoulder constantly. Things have gotten worse since Bishop started to transition into the new Don of Miami. We have enemies from all over coming out of the woodwork to try to stake their claim. You'd think after nearly twenty years of being in the game that these bottom-feeding scum would allow us to live in fucking peace as we have tried to do but nope, the cunts just keep coming.

"The cartel has made a move against us." My brows rise in surprise. I lean back in my chair and nod, we knew it was a possibility that this would happen. No one in the history of the mafia has ever taken over two states, until now.

"What did they do?" King's jaw stiffens, his eyes harden at the edges and the deadly look in his eyes has me sitting up straighter and gripping the armrests on my chair.

"They sent pictures of Nytress and Unique to Bishop." Anger burns hot through my veins.

"They're fucking dead–"

"Rook and Clare just pulled them out of school, they're back home with their parents. But, we need to get back there now. He needs you, Knight. Bishop and Gage can't get through to him." He doesn't need to say more, I'm on my feet and rushing out the door with him hot on my heels. Rook and I are closer than the others. He's my twin and if Bish and the others can't get him to calm down, then that means he needs me.

I break every speed limit to get home, King tailing me the whole way and running every red light as I do. The moment we pull up out front of Rook's house, I slam the car into park and jump out. I spot my wife on the porch with Kiara, Anya, and Destiny. Koby nods once telling me it's okay to go inside. I do just that. The moment I open the door and break through the threshold with King on my heels, I hear shouting coming from the living room.

"Fuck you! How would you feel if it was Royal or what if it was Destiny?" I round the corner to find Rook facing off against our brothers, Gage and Bishop. I spot Ally, Vin, and Car across the room with Unique and Nytress tucked into each of their aunt's sides. Vin shoots me a look, urging me to get my twin under control. Stepping forward, I cut in front of Gage and Bishop, keeping my back to them. Rook's eyes narrow in warning but I ignore it as I reach out cautiously and place my hands on top of his shoulders.

"You have my word, brother, we will deal with these cartel scum." His nostrils flare. "We will never allow them to come close to our nieces, I swear to you–"

"They can't take them, Knight. I won't let my daughters suffer the same way I did... I won't survive that shit." Pain blooms inside my chest at the reminder of what he went through all those years ago. The scars of his past still linger and the only one who is able to bring him back from the brink of despair is his wife. The imploring look in his eyes guts me, and anger begins to boil inside me as the memory of how helpless I felt at that time comes to the surface. I never want to feel that way again.

I won't fucking allow that shit to happen again!

"I'd burn the whole fucking country to the ground before I let any cunt near my nieces," I seethe.

"No one will ever touch them, brother, you have my fucking word!" The conviction in which Bishop says that alerts us all to the fact he means what he says. "I love my son, but I also love each of these fucking kids like they are my own. Do not ever question that shit again because I would lay down my life for any of them in a fucking heartbeat."

Rook takes a shuddering breath and tries to calm himself down. I shoot a look at King telling him without words to get Clare.

"I want them dealt with, but until that time I want 'round the clock security patrolling the grounds, none of the kids or the girls go anywhere without at least two men." Bishop nods his agreement.

"What about Chanel, Royal and the twins?" comes from Vin. Fuck, the four of them are away at college in Nevada. Usually, Amelia would be away as well but she is about to graduate and is home with us.

"They will be here in a couple of days, no need to alarm them. The four of them are already stirring up trouble and won't allow anyone to get the jump on them." A sense of pride washes over me. My boys are fucking tough. I knew they wouldn't listen to their uncle and hold off. Bishop may try to jerk the leash he thinks his son wears but the truth is, Royal already started making moves behind his father's back years ago.

Watching Chaos and Havoc in their element playing ball brings a smile to my face. It still shocks me twenty years later that I am lucky enough to call them mine. These two never stop making me proud. I know Chaos wants to go pro and I'm all for that but Havoc, I see myself in him and I can tell there is a darkness that clings to my son. Royal, Chanel, Destiny, Nytress and Unique play alongside their cousins in the backyard tossing the ball around.

"He got an offer." I pull my gaze from my boys and look up at my wife as she tries to sit in the seat beside me but a growl tumbles from my lips. Smirking, she quirks a brow and perches on my lap where I lock my arms around her waist and breathe her in. Fuck, even after all these years she still gets me fucking hard without even trying. She leans back and rests her head against my shoulder as she watches our boys in their element. "Chaos got an offer." I tense beneath her.

"Why do you sound so uncertain? Isn't that what he wants, to be drafted?" One thing about my wife is that she will murder anyone on her best day but fuck with her boys, she will peel the fucking skin from your flesh and smile as she does it.

"Havoc won't cope without him." Gripping her chin I turn her to face me. Her eyes say what she isn't, she's worried about our son.

"What's really going on, killer?"

"You know that they aren't waiting for Bishop to

hand things over to Royal anymore, right?" Frowning down at my girl, I shake my head.

"What are you saying, baby?"

"You heard about the heirs to the other families going missing and corrupt politicians that just vanished?"

"Yeah..." I let my sentence trail off, not sure where the fuck she is going with this shit.

"Playboy, open your eyes and think about it for a moment. The heir to the Columbian cartel went missing three weeks ago from Nevada and now, they are sending threats our way because they think it was us." I search her gaze for a moment, trying to figure out what she is meaning and then it clicks. My brows raise as I look from her to the twins and then back again.

"*Memento Mori...*" I breathe out, finally putting the piece of the puzzle together. Her eyes bore into mine.

"They have no idea that I know. They came back earlier because Ally told them about the girls. It was their first fuck up..."

"What was the second, baby?" I urge her.

"The calling cards they leave behind. The four of them have always loved playing since they were younger, it's only fitting that be their sign." I look at my twins and then at my only nephew before finally settling on my sister's only kid, seeing them all in a new light. We thought they weren't ready, and tried to shield them from the harsh reality of this life and what it holds for them. We should've known better.

Royal is exactly like Bishop, Chanel is equal parts her mother and father, and Havoc and Chaos are so different yet so similar. Chaos may look more like me but he is his mother through and through. Havoc, he's exactly like me. I see the same darkness that used to cling to me in his eyes. I don't know why that look is there but it has worried me since he turned seventeen. I know something happened but the four of them are so close none of them would dare break his trust and tell us.

"They are the Memento Mori and their calling is the cards. The cartel is after us because they think they took out the heir of their family." I stare at her in disbelief. "They are smarter, stronger, wiser and I dare say more ruthless than their parents. The four of them are going to rule this fucking world and I pray for mercy for anyone who stands in their way."

My wife has never spoken truer words.

Gage, King, Rook, Vincent and I all stand in Bishop's office, while the Don sits behind his desk with a strained look on his face.

"The Vargas cartel is coming after us because they think we had something to do with the disappearance of their heir who was studying here in the States." Bishop's words have a pit of dread settling inside me and Koby's earlier declaration coming to the forefront of my mind.

They are the Memento Mori and their calling is the cards. The cartel is after us because I think they took out the heir of their family.

What if she is right and our children did this?

"We never fucking touched their kid. They know we don't go after women or children," King snaps.

"The only way we stop them from coming after us is either fight or find the kid." Bishop's tone is ominous. The easier choice would be to find the kid but doing that shows weakness on our part, making us look like we are scared of a war, which we aren't.

"Do you have an idea about what happened to the kid?" Vin asks.

Bish shakes his head. "I knew the kid was here but I never bothered with it because they agreed to only send two guards with him. I gave them my word we wouldn't go after their kin."

"Fuck, if we go to war we risk casualties... if we don't we look like bitches." Gage voices what we are all thinking.

"I don't relish the idea of going to war but I also refuse to take the blame for harming a fucking child. We are a lot of things but we aren't kiddy killers." Looking over at Rook I can tell from the look in his brown eyes that he will ride with us no matter what we choose, even if he hates the idea. He never wanted kids or a family, much like me, but now that he has them, he will do anything to keep them safe, as we all would.

"I'll look into the kid while you get shit into motion for the upcoming war." Vin looks to each of us before settling his gaze back on Bishop with a firm look on his face. Vin may be the oldest out of all of us but the fucker hasn't aged a day, not a single gray fucking hair! "I'll fight with you as I have always done but *my* wife stays the fuck out of this and so does my daughter. I'll be sending them both to our house in Aspen where they will remain until this shit is finished. I will never allow either of my girls to be used against me."

Bishop eyes our brother-in-law warily as he pushes to his feet. Even as he has gotten older, Bish still looks like a fearsome fucker and one look from him can make a grown-ass man piss himself. For twenty years we have busted our asses making sure that everything here in New York runs smoothly since we took over from the other families, well all of them except for the Murelo's of course.

"Get my sister on the next plane out of here with my wife and the others, the cartel is coming to us," Bishop grits out through clenched teeth then drops a stack of Polaroid pictures on the small table in the middle of the room as he stalks out.

We all move toward the table and anger burns hot through my veins at the sight in front of me, each of the girls is pictured and so are the kids well, all of them except for four.

Royal,

Chanel,

Havoc,

Chaos,

Now I know without a doubt that the four of them are somehow right in the center of this cluster fuck.

Chapter Three

King

THE MOMENT I SAW MY WIFE AND DAUGHTER IN those pictures I knew that meant war, a threat like this cannot go unanswered. They came for our family and now, we will come for every single one of them, anyone who shares their blood or anyone who meant a fucking thing to them will be buried in the hole right next to their fucking corpse.

"There is no way I am leaving!" I look at Ally and sigh, knowing she wouldn't go easily. She may look like a meek little mouse but my wife is one feisty badass who isn't afraid to fuck shit up. "We have the shelters, the women rely on us–."

"I know!" I cut in. "We'll get people to take over for you, Kiara and Koby while you are gone but I cannot fight this fucking war while I am worried about you and our daughter getting caught in the crossfire."

Her gaze softens as she closes the space between us and places her palms flat against my chest peering up at me with those big blue eyes. "Our little girl just graduated yesterday, she is about to start her residency at a hospital in Chicago, we can't do this to her."

Her reasoning is solid and under any other circumstances I would agree with her but I can't, not this time. Those cunts were able to get close enough to my wife at the grocery store to snap a picture and close enough to my daughter at school—I won't let these bastards live, I can't.

"I hear what you are saying, I understand it but fucking hell, Ally." I grip her face between my hands and lean my forehead against hers, breathing her in. She is my fucking world, and the thought of ever losing her or our daughter shreds my insides. "I can't lose my girls, baby," I whisper.

Tears cloud her vision as she holds my gaze. Reaching up, she grips my forearms and implores me with a look to understand that she is more vital than I give her credit for. I know she isn't weak, she is the strongest person I know and can hold her own against a grown ass man but it isn't her job to fight. It's my job to protect her so she never has to feel the need to throw another punch. My baby girl is a sinner, that's for damn sure. Amelia hates that her mother and I are Bishop's extraction team. We will do whatever it takes to get the information Bishop needs from someone. We hurt, maim, tear them apart and then in the end, kill them.

Our daughter has dedicated her life to becoming a doctor so she can save people, unlike her parents who take lives on the regular.

"I'm not leaving you, we have faced bigger threats than this before. We will send Meelz to Aspen with the others but I'm not going. Do you understand me, King Murdoch? I am not fucking leaving you!"

The conviction in which she delivers her demand has pride swelling in my chest. Twenty years together and this woman still never stops surprising me. She is my reason for striving for more. She is perfection personified and fuck me if that shit doesn't get me rock-hard. Knowing I have an hour before I have to meet Bishop and the others, I decide to utilize that time and get reacquainted with my wife.

Gripping the back of her neck with one hand I use the other to wrap around her waist and haul her flush against me. She gasps in surprise.

"You know you drive me crazy?" I whisper as I slowly kiss along her jawline and down the side of her neck. Soft mewls and moans tumble from her sinful lips and fuck me if those sounds don't go straight to my cock.

"Y-yes." My grip on the back of her neck tightens as I lick a trail from her neck back to her lips, loving the way shudders roll through her perfect body. The moment my tongue invades her mouth, a groan pulls from deep inside me. She tastes like heaven. She grips the front of my shirt and lifts one of her legs to wrap around my waist and pulls me in closer, needing some friction against her greedy little cunt. I grip her hair and yank her back. Gasping, she stares up at me with so much need brimming in her gaze, a need she knows only I can satisfy.

"You gonna let me fuck that pussy hard, baby?"

A moan tumbles from her lips. "Fuck yes. Fuck me hard, baby, and come deep inside your pussy." I growl my approval. Ally may be a dominant woman outside of the bedroom but inside it she submits to me, knowing that her submission is always rewarded by me ten times over. I take a small step back and grip the sports bra she wears, pull it over her head and marvel at the beauty that is her full tits. My mouth waters, needing to taste these dusted pink nipples, so I do. I capture one in my mouth and flick my tongue over the enlarged nub and use my free hand to tweak her other nipple. She throws her head back and a guttural cry tears from her throat.

Switching sides I make sure to bite down softly on this side and the loud-ass moan that comes from her has my cock twitching inside my slacks.

"King, please." I release her nipple with a wet pop

and step back, holding her gaze as I begin to unbutton my shirt. Her greedy eyes feast on the small amount of exposed skin on my chest.

"Please, what?" I ask as I shrug my shirt off. She darts her tongue out to lick her lips as her gaze roams over my exposed torso. I relish the sight of her clenching her thighs together, knowing she is already dripping for me like always.

"Let me suck you." I pretend to ponder her request for a moment.

"Take your pants off and toss me your panties. If they're soaked through, then you can suck my cock. If not..." She doesn't let me finish. She shoves her pants down her legs and grabs her panties in one hand, then slowly closes the space between us. She holds her black lace G-string out to me and I snatch it from her. I bring it to my nose and inhale her heady scent, releasing an appreciative groan the moment I feel how fucking wet they are against my face. She drops to her knees and makes quick work of undoing my pants and pushing them down my legs, freeing my clock.

"Fuck, I love this cock so much, baby," she rasps out as she grips the base of my dick in one hand, then brings the head to her lips. Fuck. I will never tire of seeing this woman drop to her knees before me, the sight almost makes me come on the spot. The moment her sinful lips wrap around the tip, I throw my head and groan. She sucks me all the way to the back of her throat and fuck, I jerk in response. The sound of her gagging on my cock and the way her head bobs up and down on it is a fucking euphoric sight.

"Jesus, just like that, baby. Make your husband come." No sooner have the words left my mouth, she releases my cock with a wet pop and slowly climbs to her feet. I glare down at her in warning, she knows better than to play these games with me.

"I'm gonna need you to bury that cock deep in my weeping pussy and make me scream your fucking name so loud everyone hears it."

Fuck!

Gripping her arm I yank her forward and bend her over my desk in the study of my house. She needs no further direction as she parts her legs. Silly woman thinks she has the upper hand. I drop into my seat and pull in closer to her exposed ass and pussy, parting her cheeks. I salivate at the sight of how wet her cunt is, her arousal coating her thighs. I can't hold back, I bury my face in her pussy from behind and fucking love the sharp cry that comes from her surprise. She tastes so fucking good.

I start to fuck her greedy little cunt with my tongue. My girl pushes back against it and reaches behind herself to grip the back of my head and hold me in place as she rides my face from behind. The moment I feel her begin to tense, I yank free of her hold and lean back in my chair. She glares at me and I can't help but chuckle.

"I call the fucking shots, not you. Now bring that

perfect fucking ass back here and ride your man reverse cowgirl so I can come so fucking deep inside my pussy you'll taste me on your tonsils." Her pupils dilate and her breathing turns ragged as she quickly does as I told her. She opens her legs wide and straddles me. Gripping my cock, I line it up with her entrance and fucking groan the moment she slowly lowers that perfect fucking pussy onto my cock.

"Oh fuck," she cries out as soon as I'm balls deep inside her, throwing her head back as I grip her waist and slowly begin to guide her movements as she bounces up and down on my cock. Her greedy cunt is already gripping me so fucking hard I know I won't last much longer. This woman has a way of making me feel like a fucking pubescent teen without even trying.

I grip both her tits in my hands and knead her pert nipples as she rides me like a fucking porn star. Her movements begin to grow erratic as she chases her release. Instead of stopping this, I grip under her legs and stand. Without having to be prompted she wraps her arm around my neck for leverage, her legs spread eagle as I thrust up inside her.

"Yes, don't stop, I'm gonna come!" she shouts. My pace quickens as I drive into her harder and relish in the scream that rips from her throat the moment she clamps down on my cock and comes all over it. Four more thrusts and I'm free falling over the edge with her, roaring out her name as I empty everything I have deep inside her perfect little pussy.

Strolling into the living room of Bishop's house I feel less stressed and more level headed after my wife helped relieve some of the tension and worry I was carrying. Vin, Car and Chanel sit on one of the couches deep in conversation. I look to the left to find Rook, Clare, Gage and Anya standing near the back door speaking in hushed tones. Bishop, Knight, Koby, Kiara, Royal, Havoc and Chaos stand in the center of the room locked in a heated conversation. I peer down at Ally and quirk a brow, the tension in the room is palpable and suffocating.

"Where are the girls?" Ally asks, drawing everyone's attention to us. Amelia rounds the corner from the kitchen with an angry look on her face.

"They're at our house with Luka," Anya says. Destiny, Nytress and Unique are too young to be a part of these types of conversations.

"Why the hell do they get to sit this out and I don't?" Amelia snaps and my heart cracks. I hate that she hates this life. I know she doesn't come home often and chose the college with the best medical program, as far away from us as possible, so she doesn't need to be reminded she is a Murdoch. "I want no part of this."

"You don't get a choice in that! You are a Murdoch and you will not taint or dishonor our name by running away and getting your ass killed!" Chanel seethes. Before I can reprimand my niece, her father steps in and does it for me.

"Quiet down, Sin." She turns toward her father with an incredulous look on her face.

"Her dumbass is going to get us all killed one day or start a fucking war!" Vin opens his mouth to protest but Meelz beats him to the punch.

"I'm not your concern, Chanel! You may like what this family stands for but I don't. I save lives, not end them. Remember who the fuck you are speaking to next time you want to go off on a rant. I may not be forthcoming like you, the twins and Royal but never forget, I had the same training as the four of you growing up. I can hold my own, if need be, little girl." Shock has my mouth hanging open as I stare at my daughter. I look around the room to find everyone else staring at my baby girl like she is some foreign being.

"Well, I for one didn't think you had that bad bitch streak inside ya, cuz." Meela shoots Chaos a glare as she saunters over to her mother and me, standing a foot away, flicking her gaze between the two of us for a moment before she speaks.

"The cartel may be coming for us but I am not agreeing to get locked away at Uncle Vin's house in Aspen. I leave for Chicago in three days, and no one knows who I am, they don't even know who Royal, Chanel and the twins are thanks to Aunt Koby and Uncle Knight changing our records. We are safer back in UNLV and Chicago than we are here. Please, Dad, don't make me stay."

Chapter Four

Amelia

I stand here imploring my dad with my eyes to let me go, I can see the struggle in his gaze. The underboss in him wants to pull rank and throw me over his shoulder, then put me on the first flight to Aspen. But the father in him wants to allow his little girl to live out her dreams and be free of this life she was born into. Unlike Chanel, Royal, Chaos, and Havoc, I don't love the life we are a part of. I am doing everything I can to break away and never come back here. My family loves this life and enjoys the killing and the constant threat on their lives. I fucking hate it!

Ever since I was old enough to understand what

carrying the Murdoch name meant, I have wanted out of this place. I couldn't even go through high school or college without two guards tailing me. Shit, I had to go to school under an alias and even my residency is under my fake name. I want a normal life. I'm twenty-seven and have never been able to introduce myself to anyone by my real fucking name.

"King..." Mom looks up at Dad as she places her hand against his chest. He keeps his gaze locked onto mine as she speaks, and I make sure he can see the determination in my eyes. "You need to let her go..." No sooner have the words been uttered does Dad's angry gaze snap to her, his upper lip pulls back in a snarl. Men twice the size of my mother would be dropping to their knees and begging for my father's forgiveness just from that one look but not my mom, she matches his angry glare with one of her own.

"She's my little girl!" he roars.

Mom's brows draw in and she stands up taller. "She's not a little girl anymore, King. She is a woman and she has a life of her own. Shipping her off will force her to rebel, she barely comes back as it is." I fight the flinch that wants to break free at the hurt that laces my mom's words. I know she hates that I never come home unless I have to but I can't be a part of this world, I'm not cut out for it.

"You want me to do what, Alison? Just let my only child loose and not give a fuck that there is a threat against her? I'll kill any motherfucker who comes for my baby girl, it's my one job in this fucking wretched world to keep her safe. I failed you but I won't fail her." Mom's eyes begin to mist at the brokenness in Dad's tone. I'll admit, even I get choked up. I know my dad hates himself for what happened to my mom years ago. She was open with me about it when I got older and asked why she and my aunts ran shelters. My mom is my fucking hero.

"Bullshit!" I grit out, both my parent's gazes snap to me. "I know you would have done everything to get Mom back and you did, but I'm not her, Dad. I want something different than she does. Please, don't make me stay," I beg.

Dad reaches out and cups my cheek, his eyes boring into mine. I hate that I can see the anguish in his features. I never want to hurt my father, he is everything to me. He's the first man to love me and he will be the only man to ever know the real Amelia Murdoch. To everyone else, I am simply Max Kingsly.

"I love you, Meelz." The soft smile that spreads across his face has hope blooming inside me. "But I can't do it." I stumble back a step and his features harden. "You will be on the next flight out with the others and will remain in Aspen until I say otherwise." Anger courses through me, I wish I never had to do what I am about to but he has left me no choice. I spin around to face my Uncle. My Aunt Kiara smiles sadly at me but I focus on Uncle Bishop.

"Am I a part of the Murdoch Mafia?" He cuts his

gaze over my head to look at my father seeing if he should answer or not so I push on. "I'm asking you as the Don of the family, not as my Uncle or as my father's brother." A frown mars his face and he purses his lips. I hate that I have to put my Uncle in this position but fuck it, we all have to do things in this life that we don't like. He may not relish the fact I am putting him on the spot but, oh well. He may be the big bad Don outside of these walls but to us kids, he has always just been Uncle Bish. He never raises his voice, turns us away, or makes us feel like we don't matter, so I know without a doubt what his answer will be.

Scrubbing a hand down his face, he sighs tiredly and moves to me stopping a foot away. He places his hands on the tops of my shoulders and bends until we are at eye level. "Meelz, you know I never wanted any of you kids to be a part of this life. We all ran the risk of our kids being used against us thanks to us being who we are. I would never force you or any of your cousins into this. We were born and raised for this world, you kids were not. So, your freedom is your own and you can do with it as you please."

"Bishop–" My dad is cut off when Uncle Bish snaps his gaze to him, standing to his full height and straightening his suit jacket.

"I will not force her to stay, she is not under my rule." I wheel around and face my father ready to fight for my freedom but the moment Royal comes to stand in front of me, I clamp my mouth closed. My cousin may be younger than me but he is fucking intimidating. Unlike his father who has a way of making us feel at ease, Royal is the opposite—he is a wild card. He looms above me, his pale blue eyes bore into mine, an air of darkness clinging to him. I know he would never hurt me, but there is always this little voice in the back of my head that tells me he would murder me if I ever tried to get in his way.

"He may not force you to stay but I will." My eyes widen and my jaw unhinges in shock that Royal would speak up so openly in front of all our family.

"Royal, that's enough," Uncle Bishop warns, but he ignores his father.

"No. Her leaving paints a target on her back which then means we are splitting our resources. And if we are going to fucking war with the cartel, we need to stay together because I'm not paying a ransom for her unaware ass when she gets kidnapped."

"You're out of line, Royal," Mom says in my defense, but my cousin isn't hearing a word she says, he's too focused on getting me to submit to his demands. He inches forward a step and that's when Uncle Bishop and Dad cut in front of both me and Royal halting whatever was about to happen. Royal stands there, scowling at his father. I don't know what it is with these two but they never seem like they see eye to eye or get along. I know Royal has pulled some fucked up pranks on his father but I also know that

Uncle Bishop has tried to keep his only son away from this life.

He is a fool for not taking that gift and running—unlike me, Royal lives and breathes this life. He wants to take over from his father and run both Miami and New York. My cousin is the type to never settle. Those two places won't be enough for him, he'll want more and more and never stop until one day someone finally puts a bullet between his eyes and ends his tirade.

"You are not the head of this family–"

Royal cuts his father off. "*Yet.*" Uncle Bishop tenses and I spy his hands clenching slowly into fists at his sides.

"Learn your fucking place, boy. You may be my son but you are not the head of this family, so, until such time, you're gonna sit your spoiled ass down and shut the fuck up."

"Bishop!" Aunt Kiara scolds but she is ignored. The moment Royal steps into his father, the room stills, not a sound can be heard as we all stand in stunned silence and stare at the two men who are now chest to chest glaring at each other. If Royal wasn't his blood, I have no doubt in my mind Uncle Bishop would have murdered him years ago.

"My place is where you are standing," my cousin grits out.

Uncle Bishop pushes his forehead into his son's, baiting him to make a move. "Until my body is in the ground your fucking place is behind me, boy. Keep pushing me and I'll make sure there is nothing left of this empire *I* built by the time you are of age to take over." I see Royal's eyes darken and the pit in my gut tells me if I don't defuse this thing between them now, shit is about to change and none of us are ready for the power exchange to happen between these two yet.

"I'll stay!" I shout. I feel my father's gaze on me but I don't stop staring at my uncle and cousin. It takes a tension-filled moment before my other uncles and Chanel crowd around the duo. Uncle Rook tries to pull Royal but he shakes him off. Before the others can get to him, Chanel rushes forward, then out of nowhere Havoc and Chaos are there, helping her pull him back. The instant they are separated I start to feel like I can finally breathe again.

Feeling utterly defeated, I turn away from everyone and stalk into the kitchen pissed off at myself for giving into the demands of my family once again. When will I ever get to live my life?

So many of my friends are able to travel, have a weekend away at their family's cabin and let loose, get drunk and sleep around. I can't do any of those things, if I go away the place has to be scouted by my dad's security team and I have to have at least two guards with me at all times. I can't go to parties in case somehow someone has figured out who I really am and spikes my drink to use me as leverage against my family. Jesus, I can't even fuck a guy. Not because I can't but because I don't want to. Sleeping with someone means feelings get involved and there is no way I can bring an innocent person into my fucked up family.

"Meela?" I keep my back to my mom as I grip the edge of the counter praying for calm. I know this isn't her fault but it's hard not to blame her. "Can you talk to me, I might be able to help?" That's it, I wheel around on my mom and can't keep the anger off my face.

"How can you help, Mom? There is nothing you can do to stop me from being a Murdoch, it's in my veins and no matter how many lives I try to save someone, or what good I do in this world it will never erase the fact that I am my father's daughter." My mother's face falls at my angry declaration. I fucking hate hurting her but what did she expect?

"Amelia." I dart my gaze over my mother's head to see my dad and Aunt Koby standing a few feet behind my mom.

I throw my hands in the air and shake my head. "What are you going to do, Dad? Find another guard to act as a college student and hope I don't fuck this one or are you going to lock me in my room?" Dad's face turns an angry shade of red. He hates when I bring up the past. He hired a guard behind my back and had him enroll in the same college as me, acting like a student so he could keep an eye on me. What he didn't expect was for me to fall for my guard and sleep with him. When he found out, he lost his shit and I never saw my guard again. That is the reason I have fucking trust issues.

"I'm not going to do either of those things but what I won't allow to happen is for you to speak to your mother that way. You're angry at me, not her, so take all that anger out on the right person."

My brows raise and a sly smirk crosses my face. "Uncle Rook?" I call out.

"Meela, no," Aunt Koby warns, but I pin my aunt with a look that has her shaking her head and fighting not to smile. "Oh, yeah, she really is like you, King." Dad frowns but says nothing as Uncle Rook enters the room.

"What's happening?" he asks as he darts his gaze from his wife to my parents, and then finally settles on me.

"Dad said I can take my anger out on him." My father pales as realization dawns on him at what I have planned.

"Amelia, I won't do it–"

I cut him off. "I need the key to your gym, Dad and I are gonna go three rounds in the ring." My uncle's brows jump to his hairline.

"Uh, I don't think... Meela, you won't win." Aunt Koby snorts and pins her husband with an incredulous look.

"I beg to differ. Anya, Kiara, Carlina, Ally and myself all trained that girl how to fight. If they go at it, my money is on my niece." I shoot my aunt a grateful smile.

"I'm not going to fight my own fucking daughter," Dad snaps.

"I volunteer to take his place." I spin around to see Chanel waltzing into the room with a shit-eating grin on her face.

"No," Dad growls, but we both ignore him. Chanel doesn't stop until we are an inch apart. I look my cousin over and can tell in her mind she has already won this fight. That's okay though, I'm used to being underestimated, I have been my whole life.

"We can't leave, Bishop has the compound on lockdown," Uncle Rook says.

"We gloving it?" Chanel asks.

"Nope, meet me in the backyard in ten minutes," I grit out. We ignore the protests of everyone behind us as we lay out our terms.

A cruel smile crosses her beautiful face. "We tapping or knock out?"

"Knock out," I say with such conviction that the smile on her normally unreadable face falters slightly. None of my cousins have ever seen me fight, they all think I ran off to med school and stopped training, but I didn't. I may not be able to hack and all that other shit like them but I can fight better than all of them. Chanel is a dead shot, there is no question about that, but she lacks the stamina to go three five-minute rounds in the ring. "This will only happen once, cousin," I warn. "*When* I win, you, Royal and the twins are to get the hell off my back and stop giving me shit for not wanting to be a part of this life."

She darts her gaze over my shoulder and I have no doubt that Royal, Havoc and Chaos are now in the room and she is seeking out their agreement.

A second later she answers, "Deal. But, after I win you have to agree to stop acting like you aren't a Murdoch and start being more present in our family... because like it or not, Amelia, that is what we are, family."

Chapter Five

Gage

How the fuck did we end up in the backyard in the middle of a crisis watching our nieces fight?

Don't get shit twisted, I always knew my family was fucked up but this is a whole new level of fucked. I look around at the others wondering which one of their parents is going to step forward and stop this madness. We are family and we don't fight amongst ourselves. We are supposed to be a united front! I look across from me and shoot Kiara a look imploring her to get Bishop to step in and stop the girls from beating the shit out of each other.

"You can't stop it." I look to my side and purse my lips

at my wife, who keeps her gaze focused ahead on the girls.

"We shouldn't be allowing this shit to happen. They are family and this isn't what we do." She turns to me and I freeze at the look in her blue eyes. She turns to face me and rests her hand flat against my chest.

"Baby, this isn't how you and your siblings did things but this is their way of doing things."

"You're okay with our nieces beating the shit out of each other but the thought of our daughter wanting to go pro for the MMA you're against?" Her eyes narrow, warning me not to push her on this. Fuck that. I grip the back of her neck and pull her against me until our foreheads touch, my other hand gripping her ass, drawing a shocked gasp from her. "She doesn't want to be a lawyer, baby, she wants to fight," I whisper.

A whoosh of air escapes her. "I know. I hate that I can't support her but she is all I will have, Gage. I can never carry a child and I could never ask Vincent or Carlina to do what they did for us again."

It grates on my fucking nerves that even after all these years my crazy, stunning, badass, loving, murdering machine of a wife still harbors feelings of guilt for not being able to carry a child for us on her own. Carlina offering to carry a child for us was a gift so selfless I didn't know how to thank my sister for doing what she did. Watching my daughter grow inside my sister was bitter sweet, did I wish it was my wife carrying our daughter?

Fuck yes. But, the truth is, I don't care who carried Destiny. At the end of the day, watching her be brought into this world was a gift I will never forget. Anya, Vincent, Carlina and me were a team that day. My brother-in-law is just as selfless as my sister, never once batting an eye or making us feel a certain way for his wife carrying our daughter.

"She is all *we* need. Let go of all that guilt you carry around. All I need is you and our daughter but you can't allow your worries to hold her back. She wants to please you and with that, she will give up her dream of MMA to become a lawyer, because it's what you want."

She grips the front of my shirt in a tight hold and stares directly into my eyes. "I'll agree to this only if you are the one to train her. I trust no one else with our daughter's safety except for you and me." My smile is wide but she isn't done laying down the law. "You keep her safe, do you hear me. Anything happens to her, Gage, and I'll show you how us Russians hide a body and get away with murder." Laughter bubbles out of me.

"Baby, you know it makes me hard when you go all Russian Bratva on me." She rolls her eyes and tries to pull away but I capture her lips in a kiss to remind her I fucking own every inch of her, and there is no me without her by my side.

"You girls don't have to do this." I draw back at the sound of Ally's plea. I spin Anya around so her back is to my chest and my arms are draped over her shoulders. I thrust my hips forward and relish in the gasp that escapes her when she feels my hard cock push into her lower back.

"Your aunt is right, let's stop this," Car tries to reason with the girls, but they ignore her. Vin and King step up to each of their daughters and speak in hushed tones. I look to Ally and Carlina and find them both glaring at their husbands until King and Vin switch, both their faces slacken at the sight. I watch as Vincent begins to mimic a fighter throwing a punch, King bounces on the spot as he says something to Chanel.

Kiara comes to stand beside us and I smile down at my sister-in-law. We have a crazy past and a weird relationship. I know that it used to bother Bish but nowadays, he is content and knows she only loves him.

"Not into this, princess?" I ask.

Her shoulders deflate and she shakes her head. "No. I hate the divide between the kids. Destiny, Nytress and Unique have all clicked and love the hell out of each other. Havoc, Chaos, Sin and Royal are thicker than water. Then Meelz is on her own and I hate that." I've never paid much attention to the dynamics of the kids but now that she has pointed it out, I can't help but notice what she says is true—there really is a huge divide.

"That's because the three younger ones have no idea about this life... Those four thirst for the power this family name brings," my wife states. "Amelia has always been different from the others." Both Kiara and I frown as we follow Anya's gaze to the twins and Royal who all crowd in around Chanel while Vin and King step back, leaving Amelia on her own. "See, they may not show it but the four of them are a closed unit because they are intimidated by Meelz's strength to branch out and want something different for herself than what she was born into."

"Why do I suddenly feel like I have done my son a disservice now?" Kiara mutters. Anya pulls out of my hold and turns to face her sister-in-law, clasping her hands in her own.

"You raised that boy to be the man he was meant to be," my wife says with such conviction that pride swells in my chest. "Royal is who he is meant to be. He will honor his father's legacy better than Bishop could have ever hoped."

"But they fight so much and never seem to see eye to eye."

"Kiara, they are cut from the same cloth. That is always going to happen and there isn't a thing you can do about it. Bishop is used to everyone following his orders and fearing him. Shit, even his own brother's bow down to him." I bristle at her barb but remain silent because she isn't wrong. "Royal doesn't adhere to the same set of rules as everyone else. He is a Don in the making and whether Bishop likes it or not, his son will become his successor and take over this family, then lead it into the next generation. You raised the future king, be proud of that." Her words seem to hit their mark and have Kiara smiling. I see some of the tension from a moment ago bleed away to gratefulness that she did a good job raising her son.

"You have three rounds–" Our attention is drawn to the center of the yard at the sound of Rook's voice.

"I only need one," Chanel grits out. Amelia just shakes her head and grips the hem of her shirt and pulls it over her head so she stands in her sports bra and spandex shorts. Chanel is dressed the same. But my eyes zero in on the tattoo on Amelia's ribs, *Η ελευθερία είναι δική μου*. I have no idea what it means. I can tell it's Greek. I look to King to see his eyes narrowing, he had no idea his daughter had a tattoo either.

"Right, well, let's just remember that we are family and that—" Rook doesn't get a chance to finish before Chanel is charging Amelia. I tense, waiting for Chanel's jab to make contact, but it doesn't. Meelz ducks down and swipes her leg out causing Chanel to land face first into the grass. Amelia, smirks down at her cousin who glares up at her. Sin hates losing and we all know that. She kicks up and lands on her feet. Amelia stands still and keeps her hands at her sides. I eye her and the way she stands still and unmoving, an easy target if you will, but I know her fighting tactics. I trained all of these kids along with my brothers, Amelia has clearly been training somewhere else and that doesn't sit well with me.

Chanel charges her cousin going in for the easy hit, except at the last second Meelz throws up a block and then it's all on. The girls circle each other trading blow for blow, some make contact and some don't. Chanel switches it up when she kicks out and lands a hard blow to Meelz's side, causing her to cry out in pain. Her guard drops, Chanel sees her opening and uses it to her advantage as she lands a left hook to Amelia's face. She stumbles backward, clutching her side hunched over. Chanel allows her a moment to breathe through the pain.

"End it, now," Royal calls from the side.

"Take the left flank and switch to a X,Y combo!" Knight shouts. All of us turn to him, my mouth dropping open in shock. I knew it! He's been training Amelia without us knowing. Meelz nods at him, then straightens. She closes her eyes for a second and inhales. Chanel comes at her and I tense thinking she is about to get knocked out. Meelz eyes snap open at the last second and she reels back just as Chanel's fist skates past her face.

A whoosh of air escapes me, that hit would have caused damage if it had landed. Meelz bounces from her right foot to the left and ducks down landing a solid quick six jabs to her cousin's sternum. Sin whines in pain as she stumbles backward. Meelz gives her a chance to recover, then she pounces, landing two kicks to her left side before following up with a jab, hook, jab combo to Sin's face, then goes in with a kill combo.

She lands another two hits to her left flank, forcing Chanel to drop her guard and cover her side. Then the blow comes, her arm is cocked back ready to deliver a knockout hit. Chanel's eyes are wide, she knows she is about to be put to sleep but before Amelia's fist makes contact she freezes a millimeter away from her cousin's face breathing hard. We all gasp at the sight, Sin's eyes are scrunched shut as she waits. It takes a second for her to slowly open her eyes and the sight of Meelz's fist suspended right in front of her face has her eyes widening in surprise.

"The four of you have always doubted me and my loyalty to this family. That shit stops now," Amelia growls as she drops her arm back to her side and steps back. Royal, Havoc and Chaos rush over to Sin and help her stand upright before they all look to Amelia with angry looks on their faces. "I may not want to murder and sell guns for a living, but that doesn't mean that I won't do what needs to be done for this family. I am quiet and I do want out of this life but that doesn't mean I can't hold my own should I be kidnapped," she snarls as she looks at Royal. "You forget, I have trained longer than all of you and know more about this lifestyle than any of you, so, the next time you want to come for me, remember this moment, because next time, I won't stop." She doesn't wait for a reply as she turns and storms inside. King and Ally chase after their daughter while we all stand here in shock.

"How many times have I told you that your cockiness is going to get you killed?" Vin snaps at his daughter, Chanel turns and glares at her father.

"Maybe if you hadn't forced me to train elsewhere I would have learned that." I've never seen Vincent get mad at my sister or his daughter, but right now, he can't mask his anger to save his own ass.

"Because you are reckless!" he shouts. Car stands beside her husband looking at their daughter with a disapproving look. Fuck, I expected her to go off at Vin but the fact she seems just as pissed tells me my niece has fucked up before and still hasn't learned from that mistake. "You don't fight for the hell of it, you do it to survive! You just fought your cousin to prove a point when there wasn't a point to be made, Chanel."

"Yes, there was. She wants to turn her back on who we are and what we are. She doesn't get to do that. We are blood and if she wasn't family, she would know who the Memento–"

"Enough!" Royal cuts in forcing Chanel to clamp her mouth closed and stay silent. "This won't happen again. We'll fall into line and do what is asked of us. You have my word, Uncle Vin." I spy Bishop across from me frowning at his son. If Royal thinks he's slick trying to keep the other three quiet to hide whatever he is trying to keep hidden, then he is stupid. Bishop knows something is up and he won't give up until he uncovers whatever it is they are hiding.

"Take your cousin inside and get her cleaned up, son," Kiara says. The boys do as they are told and help Sin inside. The moment the back door closes behind them, we all huddle in close. The anger radiating off Vin can be felt by us all and it's unnerving to see the old fucker so pissed.

"We find this fucker making threats and take them out, then we focus on whatever the fuck those four are up to. Royal is acting too fucking cocky, I want to know why," Bish grits out. I cock my head to the side when I see him gnawing on his bottom lip. Koby elbows him in his side and I narrow my eyes when he flicks his gaze up to meet mine. A look of unease flickers through his eyes. I push through the center of this makeshift circle until I am standing in front of him. The bastard tries to square up for a fight but I scoff and shake my head.

"Calm down, asshole, if I wanted to beat your ass I know I have to go through your wife." My jibe earns a laugh from Koby but he just snickers. "What do you know?"

"Nothing," he bites out.

"What the fuck is going on?" Comes from Rook, who of course comes to stand beside his twin. If you fight with one twin then you best believe the other isn't far away. Even as old as they are, they still stick close to each and honestly, I find it endearing.

"Ask the dark Knight. He seems to know something about the kids he isn't sharing." At my comment I feel the others pull in closer.

"If you know something about my daughter, I want to know," Carlina demands.

"Tell us what you know, Knight," Bishop demands.

Knight sighs and shakes his head before looking at his wife. She gives him a curt nod before he runs his gaze over each of us, then settles it on Bishop.

"You remember how we heard about those heirs and politicians going missing?" Bishop frowns as he tries to recall the conversation. It takes him a minute before he nods and says,

"Yeah. What the fuck does that have to do with my son?"

"No one has been caught for those crimes, all they found were cards, right?"

"Yes, a king of clubs, queen of hearts, jack of spades and ace of diamonds," Clare supplies, and Knight nods.

"They are the calling cards of the Memento Mori," Knight says. I scrunch my face in confusion.

"The what?" Vin asks.

"It's Latin for, *remember you must die.*"

"What the hell does that have to do with our kids?" Kiara snaps as she slips up beside Bishop and interlocks her fingers through his.

"The only evidence they found were the cards at each of the scenes with the words Memento Mori etched into the backs of them. We believe that Havoc, Chaos, Chanel and Royal are the ones behind Memento Mori." My brows hit my hairline at Knight's declaration. If what he says is true, then that means the kids have defied a direct order from the Don and formed a *family* of their own.

"Fucking hell! If that's true then that means they are the ones responsible for the heir of the Vargas going missing," Anya breathes out.

"If this is true, they just started a war with the biggest crime family in Columbia," Bishop grits out.

Dread begins to pool inside me. I have a gut feeling something really bad is about to happen.

Chapter Six

Chanel

"Get the fuck off me," I snap as I shove Royal away from me. His eyes darken but he knows better than anyone not to fucking push me when I'm like this. I may have lost the fight but that isn't why I'm fucking pissed. My dad had no fucking right to air my shit out in front of everyone. I may be a disappointment to him and my mom, but that doesn't give them the fucking right to put my shit out there for my aunts and uncles to know.

"I need to check to make sure she didn't break your ribs!" Royal snarls, the sound of a snort from the doorway draws our attention. The twins turn and peer over the back of the sofa they sit on in the games room. The moment they see who it is, they are on their feet and standing on either side of me and Royal. Amelia just shakes her head and saunters into the room like we all aren't ready to hand her the ass beating she deserves. She stops a couple inches away from me and bends so she can inspect my side. The moment she darts her arm out I jump back a step and glare at her.

"What the hell do you think you're doing?" I grit out.

"I was going to check if they were broken but from the way you just hopped like a rabbit, I can tell you know they aren't." The smug lilt to her voice pisses me off.

"I don't need shit from you," I grit out through clenched teeth.

She straightens and rolls her eyes. "Maybe not but still, I just wanted to make sure you were okay," she says with a shrug. How does she not see the divide between her and us? She wants out and to live a normal mundane life working until she passes out, while we want to rule and take over the fucking world. We thirst for power, while she squanders her life away studying to save people.

"Why'd you pull the punch?" Havoc asks. I want to be pissed he brought that up but truth is, I want to know the answer to that question as well.

She rolls her lips over her teeth and shoots me an apologetic look as she answers, "Because I never want to hurt any of you. I know you four judge me because of what I want out of life and I get it, but no matter what I do or where I go, you four will always be my family. If you ever need me, just call and I'll be there. I swear." She doesn't wait for a reply as she turns and leaves us standing here, reeling.

"That girl is just as fucking confusing as a Sudoku puzzle," Chaos whines before reclaiming his seat on the couch. Havoc follows his brother as he always does, if Chaos takes a shit then you best believe Havoc is taking a shit as well. They should have been conjoined twins.

"You need to let that shit with her go, now," Royal says as he turns and peers down at me with that look. It's a look I've come to hate. It's the one where he can see inside my deepest insecurities. He will never say it aloud but he knows why I am this way with her without me needing to say it. "She is our blood. We look after our own."

I ignore him as I turn and head for the bathroom down the hall to inspect the damage alone. The moment I close the door and lock it, I flinch.

Fuck!

The bitch can throw a hit, that's for sure. I never expected that from her. I push off the door and stand in front of the mirror. My side is already bruised, my face isn't much better, but it does bring me satisfaction to know she is sporting bruises on her own face. I gently press my fingers against my ribs and hiss, the pain has my head spinning and the need for me to clutch the side of the basin to remain on my feet.

How the fuck could I allow her to get the upper hand?

You're reckless!

My father's words come back to haunt me. I look at myself in the mirror and hate that I can see so much of him and my mom in my reflection. Deep down I know they are so mad at me because of the choice I have made to follow after Royal and not take the out they gave me to study abroad and get out of this life. My mother hated being in this house and growing up a captive but I don't. My dad fought his whole life and wants something different for me, but can't they see I don't want what they do? I want this life. I want to be by Royal's side through all of this and help him lead our family into the next generation and make the changes our stubborn parents refuse to make. We will reinstall glory to our family name.

His family name.

I may be a Murdoch by blood but not by name. I'm a Murelo. Royal always says that means nothing because to him I am a Murdoch. I know me wanting to be a Murdoch hurts my father but it isn't about wanting to hurt him, I will always be a Murelo and I am proud as fuck of that. I just want to be the same as the others. Why is that so hard for him to understand?

A knock sounds at the door. I grit my teeth, thinking it's Royal, and pull it open ready to tell him to fuck off but clamp my mouth closed at the sight of my dad. He looks at me with an unreadable look in his eyes.

"Dad?" At the sound of my voice his features relax slightly but the same look in his eyes remains.

"We need to talk." Four words no daughter wants to hear. He doesn't wait for me to respond as he turns and walks away, not once checking to see if I'm following after him. We step out the front door and he walks to the end of the porch, where the rocking chairs sit. He claims one and motions for me to sit in the other. I bite down on my tongue to keep the hiss of pain inside me as my ribs begin to ache in protest. "You're as good as me with hiding your pain." I look out of the corner of my eye to see he isn't looking at me.

"How would you know?"

"You're my daughter, Chanel. I know you don't love that fact but it doesn't make it any less true." Sighing I recline back in the chair and look out over the houses down the hill. Uncle Bish wanted his family close so he built all his siblings houses and made a community of his own. That is pretty fucking cool if you ask me.

"I don't hate being your daughter."

"Then why are you trying so hard to be a Murdoch? You don't have to try, Chanel, you are one of them by birth."

"I'm not trying to be anything. I'm just doing what I'm supposed to do," I defend.

"So, telling people your last name is Murdoch instead

of Murelo is the way to do that?" The hurt that laces his voice has me feeling guilty.

"It has nothing to do with being ashamed of where I come from or what my name is. Just so we're clear, I have never introduced myself as a Murdoch or a Murelo. We may have alluded to who we are and where we come from but we have never openly admitted that shit out loud, we're not that stupid," I snark—he thinks I'm an idiot.

"How did you go from wanting to be with me all hours of the day to not even wanting to sit next to me and have a conversation?" I lull my head to the side to find my dad staring directly at me. I hate that I see hurt in the depths of his eyes. How do I explain this to him?

"I... I..." The sound of shouts coming from inside has us both climbing to our feet heading back into the house. The moment we round the corner to the living room, I balk at the sight of Royal and Uncle Bishop shouting at each other while Aunt Kiara stands in the middle of them.

"You don't know shit, boy!"

"Oh and you do because you're the fucking Don?" Royal laughs, but there's no humor to it. "Go on then, old man, pull that side piece out and force me to my knees, make me submit." I know my cousin and I can tell he is a couple seconds away from unleashing all the fury he has buried for years.

"Don't you fucking dare!" Aunt Kiara warns her husband.

Uncle Bishop scoffs. "You think you can do a better job, is that it?" I plead with Royal silently not to take the bait his father has just laid for him, but he's too pissed off to see reason and falls for it.

"Yes, I do."

The smile that graces my uncle's face at his answer has me tensing. "Oh, okay then. Well then allow me to pass this piece of knowledge onto you then, son. When you become Don, you don't get to hide behind a deck of cards." My eyes widen for a second before I school my features. I look across the room to see Havoc and Chaos staring at me. I give them a subtle shake of my head. They can't prove shit unless Royal owns up to it but he won't. "You also can't call yourself the reminder of death because you become the Grimm fucking Reaper when you are Don."

Royal has a huge ass ego and I know his dad taunting him like this is hard, but he needs to keep his cool or he will blow up everything we have worked our asses off to achieve.

"Oh shit," Royal says as he takes a step back and laughs. I keep the frown off my face as I look at the twins who both stare at Royal with unease. Our cousin is a crazy son of a bitch and at any moment he can go from kind and caring to full on psycho mode in less than a second. "You think we are those little bitches out in Nevada leaving the calling cards?" He laughs again but this time there is humor to it, I get it. He's playing it all off so they don't catch on, he's fucking brilliant. Judging from the look on his father's face, he isn't sure if the information he has been given is true or not now.

"We know it's you," Uncle Bishop snaps.

"Oh, well, please tell me how the four of us have time to study, play sports, train and then go out and make people disappear all in a day's work?" The sarcasm is thick in my cousin's voice.

"I mean it, Royal, if you took the fucking heir I need him back."

"Why?" That one word holds more power than my uncle would like. None of my other uncles or aunts dare interfere in this argument knowing this is nothing unusual for these two.

"Because, he is from the biggest crime family in Columbia and they are declaring war on us." I know Uncle Bishop is trying to catch Royal slipping but he won't, he's too smart for his own good sometimes.

"If I had the little bitch I would. I mean, if you want you can fly out to UNLV and check my dorm where I stash all the bodies of my victims. Or, you could check Sin's and the twins' rooms, because that's where I hide all our plans and the arsenal of weapons I get sent in from Aunt Anya's friend in Russia."

"That's enough. He said he didn't do it, Bishop," Aunt Kiara says, then turns to face her son. No matter what he does or says his mother never looks at him with anything but love in her eyes. I envy that. "You need to be telling the truth right now, Royal. If you're not, we are about to go to war with a family who has been stalking us and sending pictures of your little cousins to your father." Royal's face slackens. I gulp and the twins tense but none of us say a word.

"I didn't have anything to do with whatever happened to that kid, Mom. Ask Sin and the twins." Aunt Kiara darts her gaze to the twins, they both shake their heads. She looks to me next and I smile reassuringly, shaking my head, backing my cousin. I'll never not have his back.

She smiles sadly then steps into my cousin and rests her hand flat against his chest as she looks up into his eyes. "I gave you life. I raised you to be who you are and everything you will become." Royal frowns and looks at his father who seems just as confused as him. "You may think you are slick and can hide shit from me... and you did until I looked at your cousins. You tensed for a split second and gave yourself away." I force myself to remain calm and show no emotion on my face. I peek at the twins and see them doing the same. Royal keeps his cool and the frown in place.

"Mom, you're wrong—"

She cuts him off. "Maybe, except the entire time you have been standing here watching your father and answering his questions, I've been watching Chanel." My eyes widen in surprise. I feel my dad's stare boring into the side of my head. Aunt Kiara flicks her gaze to me and smiles. "You, my dear, are a force like your mother. I see it in your eyes, my dear niece. If Bishop had tried anything you would have fought for my son, which is why the moment the cards were mentioned, I looked to you."

"What?" I breathe out.

"They were your idea. Royal wouldn't have been able to pull any of that off without your help. I know that and so does he. Which is why I am asking you, as his mother, to help me save my son from going to war with the Vargas cartel."

I look at Royal who remains stoic and unmoving. I know his tells though. The slight crinkle in his left eye tells me to deny everything his mother is saying and not own up to shit.

"I'm sorry, Aunt Kiara, I don't know what you're talking about—"

Before I can finish my mother cuts in, "Chanel, now is the time to be truthful. Your family needs your help."

I can't contain the snort that comes out as I look across the room to my mother who stands between her twin brothers. "That's rich coming from you."

"Chanel!" my father warns, but I ignore him.

"No, she wants me to be perfect and run away from my family and yet, she stands there claiming they need my help?"

The front door slams open drawing all our attention

to Luka and four other guards entering the room. Uncle Bishop and Royal immediately place themselves in front of my aunt without thought and I fucking love that *that* is their first reaction.

"Boss," Luka states.

"What is it?" Uncle Bish demands.

"We need to move on the Vargas cartel. They just blew the cargo ship that was docked there up." Everyone begins to shout and bark orders. Uncle Bishop leads my father and uncles out of the room with his men following close behind him. The power that rolls off him is addicting. I look back to my cousin to see the longing in his eyes, he wants to be a part of the action but until his father views him as an equal, he's stuck out here trying to prove himself worthy to his father, just like I am.

Chapter Seven

Vincent

WE ALL STAND AROUND BISHOP'S OFFICE AS LUKA plays the video he was sent of the Colombians blowing up one of the ships that was bringing in the guns. We had a deal with them, we traded some of the guns we got from Russia if we got some of theirs, plus we would also help them ship their coke through Anya's method that she still refuses to share with any of us.

"They just declared war." Bishop's ominous tone fills the room with a sense of dread but there is also excitement tinged with that. It's been a minute since any of us have had to use our skill sets, and I for one am ready to get back in the field and hit a target.

"So, does that mean we're giving up on trying to find their kid?" Rook asks from his place on the sofa next to King.

"We're way past making a truce now," Gage answers from his spot against the far wall. Knight stands next to me nodding his agreement.

"How long ago was that video taken?" King asks Luka.

"Twelve hours ago, so twenty minutes after it docked," he answers.

"We're not going to get an honest answer out of the kids on the whereabouts of the heir, so we need another plan now," Knight announces from next to me.

"We need to go to Colombia and take the fuckers out," Lennox, one of Bishop's men, growls.

"No, dumbass," I snarl. The fucker shoots me a glare, but the moment the barrel of Bishop's gun is shoved into the side of his head, his face pales.

"That's my brother-in-law you are looking at like that. Remember your fucking place or the next time you do that, your place will be six feet fucking deep, got it?" The weasel gulps and nods, then takes a step back the moment Bishop drops his gun back to his desk and looks at me. "What do you have in mind?"

"We need you to finish taking over Miami. They own the whole of Colombia and have allies all around South America. We need the numbers Miami affords us to go to war against them in order to make sure we come out on top with minimal casualties on our side." B nods and bites the corner of his bottom lip as starts to think up a plan.

"Okay, we need to get on a plane and get the fuck to Miami so I can lock that shit down, then we go to war," he declares.

"What about the kids and the girls?" Gage asks.

"We send them all to Aspen," Bishop says leaving no room for argument. Knight, Gage, Rook, King and me all chuckle. "What?" Bishop snaps irritated.

"If you think for a second your sister, wife, or sister-in-laws are getting on a plane you are out of your fucking mind. The only way Carlina is leaving is if I drug her and that isn't going to happen because my girl can track my ass to the end of the world just to kill me." I roll my eyes when all five of her brothers smirk. I flip the fuckers off. We stayed holed up in Bishop's office until later that evening. By the time we all come out, I'm fucking tired, hungry and ready to call it a night. King, Knight, Rook, Gage, Luka and I all make our way down to our houses. I smile at the sight of all the front porch lights on, even Luka's light is on.

"Get yourself a fucking girlfriend so my wife stops doing shit for you!" Rook forces out, earning a laugh from the rest of us.

"Dude, my sister is always going to worry about me. Plus, who says I don't got someone?" That has all of us slamming to a stop and facing Luka, who frowns. "Why are you all looking at me like that?"

"I thought you were gay." Luka reels back as if Gage smacked him.

"Why the fuck would you think that?" he snarls.

"Well, you never have a girl over and it's not like we have ever seen you with anyone so I just assumed," Gage defends with a shrug.

"Why the hell would I bring a girl back here to see all your ugly faces?" he says, and brushes past us, continuing on to his house. The five of us stand here and just watch him. Just before he enters his house he turns back to us and flips us off. The five of us laugh at his expense.

"He's so full of shit," Knight rasps out.

"Ya think?" Rook tacks on.

"There is no way he is getting laid, he doesn't have the fucking time," King adds.

"Speaking of getting laid..." I let my sentence trail off as the four of them turn to glare at me, causing me to laugh. Even after all these years, they still hate knowing I fuck their sister nightly.

"You disgust me!" Rook grits out as he storms off toward his house.

"You're a real fucking prick," Knight bites out as he follows Rook toward his own house. King and Gage just stand there shaking their heads with smiles on their faces.

"I'm too tired to defend my sister's virtue, night fuckers," King says as he follows after the twins, heading home.

"Your sister lost that shit years ago, bro," I call out.

King just flips me off over his shoulder. I shake my head and laugh as Gage and I slowly head back to our own homes.

"I have a bad feeling, Vin." I pause and turn to face him, the dreadful look on his face indicates he isn't fucking with me.

"What do you mean?"

He looks around as if to make sure no one can hear what he is about to say. "I have this feeling that something bad is about to happen. I can't explain it but I feel it in the pit of my gut." I eye him warily for a beat. Out of all the Murdoch brothers, he is the one I am closest to.

"What has you on edge about this?"

He shakes his head and scrubs a hand down his face. "Have you ever had a feeling where you know you're on borrowed time?"

Frowning, I shake my head. "Can't say that I have."

"I feel like my time is about to run out, Vincent. I feel it, like this war will be the end of me." I reach out and place a hand on his shoulder and give him a gentle shake making sure he can see the seriousness in my gaze.

"I will never let you fall, brother. I got your back, always. You will come home to your wife and daughter. I'll make fucking sure of that, you hear me?" He nods but I can see it in his eyes that he doesn't believe a word I'm saying. I'll just have to prove him wrong because there is no way I am leaving my best friend behind.

After getting something to eat, I head upstairs and go to the spare room to shower so I don't wake Carlina. After I finish up, I head for my bedroom but pause at the sound of voices. My bedroom door is slightly ajar so I peek inside to see my wife and daughter sitting on the bed with their legs crossed under them.

"I get it. What you want is different to what I want, Mom."

Car sighs and I see her shoulders deflate. "I know, baby girl. I am so sorry for not seeing sooner that you are your own person. I guess, a part of me always wanted my daughter to be like me and love the lavish things in life and enjoy getting her hair and nails done." They both chuckle. Carlina reaches out and cups our daughter's cheek as she smiles. "I get it now." Chanel melts into her mother's hold and smiles brightly. I haven't seen my daughter smile like that in years and something about the sight of it pulls at my heartstrings.

"If you can understand, why can't he?" I tense, I know the *he* she is referring to is me.

"Because he can't stand the thought of his only child wanting to become him." My brows draw in as I try to piece together what she means.

"It's because I don't have a cock swinging between my legs." I bite my tongue to keep from growling at hearing my daughter say that vulgar fucking word. I may use it and it may be fucking sexy when her mother says it but coming from her, it sounds utterly disgusting.

"That's not it at all. You being a girl means nothing to your father. He didn't care what the sex of the baby was when we found out I was pregnant. All he cared about was the fact you were healthy and would always know you are loved. He may not show it, Chanel, but you are the apple of his eye and he just wants you to be happy and safe."

"But what about what I want? He never listens, Mom. All he does is tell me I'm reckless, I could do better or that I should study more. He doesn't see me for me!" I can't take it anymore, I shove the door open, and both their heads turn toward me. Car looks surprised to see me but Chanel just looks pissed off. "Eavesdropping?"

I ignore her question. "I do see you, Chanel. I see everything there is to see about you and there isn't a goddamn fucking thing I would change about you because to me, you are fucking perfect. I know you want to hunt and do what I do, but take a second to see it from my side. You are my baby girl and you are asking me to be okay with you going out on a contract to take the life of someone else. Not all of my targets are low level. Some are mob bosses, some are under bosses and some are just downright cunts. What if one of them was to get the drop on you? How the fuck can I live without you?" I don't give her a chance to answer. "I can't! You are my fucking reason for everything that I do. Aside from your mother, I have nothing else worth living for in this world."

My daughter stares at me with an open mouth and a blank look in her eyes. Carlina smiles proudly at me. I have expressed to her many times how I feel about our only child wanting to follow in my footsteps. She agrees that the life I have chosen to live is dangerous. This isn't the type of life I want for my daughter, but the reality is, I really don't have a say in the way she chooses to live hers.

"What's so bad about me wanting to be like you?" she whispers. My shoulders sag as I run a hand through my hair trying to think of a valid response.

"Nothing is wrong with wanting to be like your father." I cut a glance at my wife and watch as she grabs both Chanel's hands and holds them in hers. "He thinks so low of himself and he expects everyone else to think that of him, but you and I get to see the real man beneath the mask he wears." I purse my lips hating that she is right but not liking that she is airing my shit out. "He doesn't worry about you because you are a girl, he worries about you following in his footsteps because you are his child. All any parent wants is to keep their children safe. With the life you want to lead, we can't guarantee that."

"I could get hit by a bus tomorrow," Chanel deadpans.

"Then I would have to murder a bus driver very fucking slowly," I growl. My daughter throws her hands up in frustration.

"You think this is a joke and never take me seriously. That's why we always fight. Uncle King and Amelia fight all the time because she hates who her father is but I don't. I am fucking proud to say my father is Vincent Murelo, that you are the Bloodhound. Your name alone instills fear into your enemies. I want that." A light bulb moment hits me.

"You don't want to be a Murdoch because you are ashamed of me, you want that name because everyone knows it and will fear it." She drops her gaze to the bed, answering my question without words. It's true, everyone knows me as the Bloodhound and not by name. The name Murelo holds no weight anymore, not after me and my brothers-in-law laid waste to my father and his men. "Chanel?" She slowly lifts her gaze back to mine.

"Yeah?"

"I can't lose you," I say honestly. Her features soften and she jumps off the bed, rushing toward me. The moment she is within reach, I wrap my arms around my little girl and hold her close. I hear my wife sniffle at the sight of us embracing. She never hugs me anymore.

"You won't lose me, Dad," she mutters against my chest.

I tighten my hold on her as I flick my eyes up to look at my wife, she nods encouragingly at me and without words tells me that I need to let her do this or I will lose my daughter and I can't stomach the thought of that. I relish in this embrace for a minute longer and then gently push her back, resting my hands on her shoulders. I bend at the knees so we are eye level.

"You do everything I say—"

"I will, I swear."

I narrow my eyes, forcing her to clamp her mouth closed. "I mean it. Everything I say you do."

"I swear, Dad. I'll do it." I fucking hate that me agreeing to teach her how to become an assassin is what brings the brightest smile to her face.

"Fine. The moment I get back from Miami with your uncles I will start training you." She squeals and hugs me again, promising that she will make me proud. Stupid girl.

You make me proud just by breathing.

Chapter Eight

Chaos

Lying here in my old room at my parent's house feels weird. I'm used to sharing with Havoc and having rotating girls come through my door each night. Havoc and I do everything together, sometimes it's hard being a twin but for the most part, I love it. Having someone always watching my six puts me at ease. He never doubts me or judges me for the choices I make. Even when I fucked up hugely, he never turned on me or called me on it when he found out.

I hate that I nearly let a bitch come between me and my brother. The girl fucked me up so badly and left me reeling. We may lie about who we are and where we come from for good reason, but she knew and she still chose to lie to me!

Loving her could have ruined my family, which is why Havoc and I went rogue and did what we did. I don't bother to tear my gaze from the ceiling when my door opens, I already know who it is.

"They're going to find out what we did." I lull my head to the side and pin Havoc with my *don't fucking test me* look. He growls and shoves off the wall as he begins to pace the length of my room. "They are coming for our family, Chaos."

I sit up and swing my legs over the side of the bed, rest my arms on the tops of my thighs and lift my head to meet his gaze. Everyone thinks Havoc doesn't feel anything and is closed off from the world. The truth is, he feels too deeply and chooses to close himself off so he doesn't get hurt.

"You say nothing, Havoc!" His brows jump to his hairline and a disappointed look overtakes his face.

"Royal is getting crucified for this when he had nothing to do with it. Jesus, if Sin finds out—" He clamps his mouth closed when I climb to my feet and get right in his face.

"You say nothing and keep your fucking mouth shut." Havoc doesn't back down like he normally does, instead, he pushes his forehead against mine.

"If it becomes a choice of saving our family or

protecting you from Royal's wrath, I'll protect the family." My eyes widen.

"You would go against me?" I can hear the shock in my own voice. Never in our entire lives have Havoc and I not been on the same page. We always have each other's backs first, no matter what.

He snaps his arm and grips the back of my neck forcing me in closer. "I will always have your back, no matter what, but if this shit blows up and it comes back on Mom and Dad and the rest of the family, I will protect them. We did what we did because of *her*. We owed her nothing and yet we still did it."

"I didn't do it for her," I growl. Havoc's eyes soften for a second before he quickly masks it.

"You keep telling yourself that."

I shove him back and spin away. As I stalk over to the window and gaze out over the backyard, guilt gnaws at me for a second before I shut that shit down. I did what I did because it had to be done.

"They have no idea that they are going to war because of us. We left Royal to hang today, Chaos." I spin around and scowl at my brother.

"You want to bitch out and go snitch?" I don't give him a chance to answer. "Go, fuck off and go tell Mommy and Daddy then, you pussy ass bitch." His brows raise and his mouth opens slightly in shock at my outburst. "You snitch and you and I are done. Don't ever come to me for shit."

He shakes his head and stares at me with wide eyes and disbelief. "Just like that, huh?"

I shrug my shoulders and stare out the window, ignoring him for a second, as I try to contain the anger brewing inside me. He has no idea what the fuck she did to me and why I needed to do what we did.

"It had to be done, Havoc. He needed to go. None of that had anything to do with who she is, everything had to do with what the fuck he did. This war that is coming, may have started because of what we did but even if we didn't do it, they were still coming for us."

"How could you know that?"

"Because she told me." I can feel his gaze drilling into the back of my head. I ignore it. He and I are one and the same, and no matter what either of us says or does, we will always protect each other.

"She's the enemy, Chaos. She nearly destroyed us once. I won't let that bitch or her family come between us again. You best come to terms with that, fast," he grits out before leaving my room. The moment the door closes, my shoulders slump. I push my window open and climb out onto the roof. Laying back, I gaze up at the stars and allow myself to imagine a life where being a Murdoch isn't a reality.

We all give Amelia shit for wanting out of this life, truth is, I want what she does but I just don't have the balls to be as vocal as she is. If I wasn't Knight and Koby Murdoch's son, I would have a chance to be something other than who I am. I would love to go pro and be drafted by the NFL. My parents support my dream but they are blinded by rose colored glasses. There is no way I will ever be drafted. As soon as they learn what my last name is, they will reject me.

"Hiding away?" A whoosh of air escapes me at the sound of Royal's voice. He climbs out my window and drops down beside me.

"How'd you get in here?"

He snorts. "Dude, your mom still doesn't lock the front door and even if she did, I would have just picked the lock." I have nothing to say to that so I just nod and continue to gaze up at the stars. After a few minutes, Royal gives in and lays down beside me, gazing up at the stars. Neither of us says anything for a long while, both of us lost in our thoughts. "Why did you lie to me?"

I look out of the corner of my eye to see he's still looking up at the night sky. "What are you talking about?"

"Lie to everyone else but me, Chaos. The moment my dad brought up the cards and the missing heir, I knew you were behind it."

Now that garners my full attention. I turn my head only to find him doing the same thing and staring directly back at me.

"You accusing me?"

Royal's composer remains calm. "No, Chaos. I'm asking you why you didn't tell me that you and Havoc disposed of the Vargas heir?" I should have known he would find out, he always fucking does. It's like his superpower or some shit.

"What do you want me to say, Royal? I made a judgment call."

"You made a shitty call, Chaos, a real shitty call."

"Oh, and let me guess you would have made a different one?"

His eyes narrow. "I would come up with an idea that didn't leave getting your ass handed to you by your dad in front of everyone. I would have made sure I was by your side the entire fucking time, but you didn't. You left me to deal with that shit on my own!"

Guilt gnaws at me. He isn't wrong, I shouldn't have let him take the blame and been man enough to stand by his side.

"You're right." He pins me with a dry stare. "How did you figure it out?"

"It wasn't hard. I knew one of you did it because of the calling card that was left. It wasn't hard to piece it together when I spoke to Sin and we figured out the night shit went down she was with me, that only left you and Havoc. We all know Havoc doesn't do shit without you, so, therefore, I knew you were the mastermind behind this."

He isn't wrong, Havoc doesn't do anything without me. He and I differ in that aspect. I can branch off and do my own thing. Havoc will just follow whatever I do. He thinks I have no idea that he's still a virgin. I mean seriously, my twin is nearly twenty-one and still a fucking virgin. The guy is going to wind up getting married in white at the rate he's going.

"I did what I had to do and I'm not sorry about it either."

Royal sighs and nods. "It was because of what he tried to do to her, wasn't it?" I grind my teeth so fucking hard my jaw aches. "You don't need to answer, the angry glint in your eyes said *yes* for you."

"Why aren't you yelling or screaming about it?"

"Because, I know you still love her even when you deny it. He wanted to marry the girl you have always pined after but because of who she is, you can never be with her."

"I couldn't watch her marry him. He bragged around campus about what he had planned for her and..." I clamp my mouth closed and scrub my hand down my face in frustration.

"You couldn't bear the thought of seeing the girl you are in love with marry someone else and know her new last name wouldn't be yours." I deflate and nod. "Is he still alive?"

"No."

Royal's face drops and resignation shines in his eyes. He and I both know I fucked up but we are family, which means he will help me no matter what.

"Can any of this lead back to us?"

I shake my head. "No."

"Where's the body?"

"At the bottom of the ocean with concrete anklets."

He snorts. "You went old school mob, huh?"

I shrug my shoulders and wink. "What can I say..." We both laugh like girls and it feels nice to finally have my secret out.

"We'll figure this out. We won't let them come after our family, Chaos. We will protect our own."

"Fucking right we will, brother," I say without an ounce of hesitation.

Chapter Nine

Havoc

I STAND HERE WITH MY BACK AGAINST THE WALL AND my window cracked open a bit. I hear everything they say on the roof and it makes me happy to know that Royal isn't pissed at Chaos for what we did. I mean, he is definitely annoyed but what can he do about it now, the guy is already dead.

I never understood why guys would get all twisted up over a female until Lailani. The girl was like a walking dream—big brown eyes, long brown hair that flowed around her like a cape. She didn't dress like the other girls in short skirts and crop tops, she covered up and left so much to the imagination that it used to drive me crazy thinking about what she looked like underneath it all. She was the first girl who had captivated my attention without even trying. It's true what they all say about me. I never do anything for myself. I always put Chaos first, no matter what, except this one time, I wanted to be selfish.

I was finally going to have something for myself. I didn't care about the consequences, I just wanted her to be mine and she was for a while until he found out. Royal and Chanel think Chaos found her first. He didn't, I did. I made sure not to tell her I was a twin because I wanted her to want me and not the both of us.

She saw me!

She didn't see Chaos's twin or the star QB's brother, she just saw me for me. She didn't want me because of the rumors of where I came from, she was real. I fell for her. She was my secret, my selfish little escape from the shadow of my twin. It all went to shit when I had to come home for a few days. I never told her I was leaving. For three days I was an anxious mess to get my ass back to UNLV and see her. The moment I landed, I didn't go to my brother or my cousins, I went straight to her dorm. The moment I burst through that door and saw her naked beneath Chaos, everything inside me died.

He never said it but I knew at that moment, he did it to make sure she couldn't take me away from him. She tried to say she never knew he wasn't me, but I didn't want to hear it. She knew me. She should have been able to tell us apart even if she didn't know we were twins. Well, that's what I keep telling myself anyway.

My phone pings and I know without a doubt that it's her. She's the only one aside from my family that has my number. I should have changed it but I'm a sucker for punishment.

LANI

You took care of it?

I debate on whether I should leave her on read or not, but the truth is, she never asked for what happened, we did it because we wanted to.

ME

It's dealt with, lose my number.

LANI

Will you hate me forever?

Hate is a word I don't use often, it seems so final. Do I despise her? Yes. Do I wish death upon her? No. I could never wish that on her even if she fucked me over. She hid who she was from Chaos, but not me. I knew from the start who she was and where she came from. I just didn't care because I wanted her.

I scoff to myself, of course the first girl I fall for my brother has to go and steal from me and fall in love with her as well.

Oh shit, did I not mention that Lailani is the girl we killed the heir for? Whoops, yup. Turns out a female really can make a man commit murder. Chaos used her to keep me with him but in the end, even he couldn't help but fall in love with the girl who owned my heart. Before I can reply, my phone starts vibrating in my hand with an incoming call. I don't think as I answer it.

"Havoc?" The sound of her melodic voice has me slamming my eyes closed and praying for strength.

"What do you want?" I clip out.

"The same thing I have always wanted," she whispers.

"Don't," I snarl.

"What do you want me to say?" I shake my head even though she can't see me.

"Nothing, there is nothing you can say."

She sighs on the other end of the phone and I hate that I stand here wishing she would just tell me a story, so I can listen to her voice and lull myself into dreaming that the past never happened and we were just Lani and Hav again.

"I'm sorry that you had to do what you did. He won't stop, Havoc."

"Your father is a cunt," I growl. She scoffs.

"Tell me something I don't know. The Vargas boy was one of many, you can't end everyone he tries to marry me off to." I frown.

"Wait, what do you mean?"

"About what?"

"I thought the heir was forcing you into marriage?"

"No, I told Chaos my father arranged the marriage so he could expand into Colombia and come for your uncle." I'm grinding my teeth so fucking hard I fear they will crack. Chaos lied to me. He told me Lailani was being forced into marriage with the heir against hers and her family's wishes. He said they didn't have the numbers to go against the Colombians so we had to help her. "Oh my God, you didn't know?"

"It doesn't matter," I force out through clenched teeth.

"Of course it does! When are you going to learn that he isn't any good for you, Havoc?" My anger starts to burn hot inside me. "Everyone thinks you are dark and closed off but the truth is, he made you like that. He is the one who can't live without you–"

"Fuck you! You don't ever get to speak about my brother like that. I'm the way I am because you fucked me over and ruined any chance I had at being happy. This is on you not him!" I end the call and throw my phone across the room and relish in the sound of it shattering against the wall. One day I am going to get my revenge on that girl and it is going to be the sweetest fucking thing I have tasted. Watching her break in front of me, will be everything I have ever wanted. I'm going to use her broken pieces to patch myself back together.

Chapter Ten

Royal

WE'VE BEEN STUCK HERE FOR THREE DAYS AND I AM about to lose my fucking mind!

I hate being back here and living under my father's rule. He thinks because he wears the title of *Don* that it makes him superior, it doesn't. He may think he is better than the rest of us but he isn't. He was just the firstborn and got to wear the crown of this family and that's it. I need a fucking drink. I make my way toward the kitchen to get a beer but as I pass my dad's office he calls out.

"Royal, come here." I slam my eyes closed and pray for patience. I fucking hate being ordered around. I enter his office and I have to admit I'm surprised to find him alone here. "Take a seat." Curiosity gets the better of me, which is the only reason I obey his command without argument. He continues to flick through a stack of papers and type away on his computer while I sit here and wait. I take the time to look him over. He's always worn suits and I don't understand why, the fucking things are so restricting. His hair is graying now but he still holds that natural don't fuck with me look on his face. I doubt that will ever go away.

When he curses beneath his breath and darts his gaze to me, something flickers in the depths of his brown eyes and it sets me on edge.

"What is it?" I ask.

He eyes me warily for a moment, something about the way he is staring at me and frowning tells me he is debating if he should share this information with me and treat me like a man or continue to keep me at arm's length and hope like hell I won't come for what is mine the moment I turn twenty-one.

"The Vargas cartel is in the US." My eyes widen in surprise, he never shares information like this with me.

"Why are you telling me?" I ask skeptically.

He sighs and rests back in his chair. "Because I've been informed they are in Miami."

"What the fuck?"

"Calm down."

"How the fuck can you sit there so calmly? They

have just shit on us by coming to our turf, we need to clap back!"

He shakes his head. "No."

"Why not?"

"Think like a boss, son. You are thinking like a soldier, not a Don, and that mentality is going to get your people killed. We need to be smart. There is an election happening in Miami right now, too many people to have a war."

"What are you suggesting then?"

"Your uncles and I will travel to Miami–"

"I'm coming."

"No, you're not." My lip pulls back in a snarl as I scowl at my father.

"Miami is rightfully mine and you can't stop me from going."

"Maybe not, but I can sure as hell have your ass tossed in the bunker and locked up until I get back."

"Mom would murder you."

He smirks cunningly. "What your mother don't know won't hurt her." My jaw locks. "I don't enjoy being at odds with you, Royal," he says after a tense minute of silence.

"It's not like you and I have ever gotten along," I bite out.

A look of sadness crosses his features. "We did, but then you grew up and wanted to become the boss. I can't give this mantel to you until you are ready, son."

I scoff and roll my eyes. "You'll never give it up, you'd rather die in that seat."

"No, I would rather die on top of your mother, but hey." I scrunch my face in disgust and shudder. The asshole throws his head back and laughs at my expense.

"That's fucking nasty!"

"No, son, that's love." I quirk a brow at him, not following where the hell he is going with this. "One day you will sit here as the head of the family. You will think you are untouchable and at the start you might be, but you will never become a true king until you have your queen by your side."

"I don't need a woman to lead," I defend.

"Maybe not, but behind every successful man is a strong as fuck woman who pushes you to be better and want more. I was nothing and fucked up leading for years until your mother came back into my life. She is the reason I was able to make this family what it is today."

Realization dawns on me. "Are you saying I have to marry in order to take over?"

He pales and shakes his head rapidly. "Your mother would fucking castrate me if I did that." I smirk knowing he isn't wrong. "All I am saying is, one day you will lead and think you are king of the world but you will realize soon enough that having this massive kingdom isn't worth shit if you don't have anyone to share it with."

The thought of settling down with a woman doesn't appeal to me. I enjoy my freedom too much to be tied down to one woman. He may feel this way and shit may have worked out for him after he found my mom, but that doesn't mean that shit applies to me.

"I know you hate me—"

"I don't hate you, Dad," I cut in. He smiles but it doesn't reach his eyes.

"Fine, I know you don't like me most of the time." I can't help the chuckle that escapes me, as the asshole grins and winks before continuing. "But, I want you to know that I am proud of you, Royal. I couldn't have asked for a better fucking son. I know I said your mother is the reason for everything but the truth is, I never knew what love really was until the moment I held you in my arms. You changed the game for me, son."

My eyes are wide and my mouth slightly ajar, I have never heard my father speak like this before. Fuck, I think this is the longest conversation we have had without fighting since I was like sixteen.

"I wanted to build a better world for you and your cousins. I did everything I could to make sure you would all be safe and no harm would ever come to any of you kids. I know you thirst for leadership and I understand that because I was the same, but until the day you become a father you will never understand what this feels like."

"What *what* feels like?" I whisper.

"Fear." I frown and cock my head to the side. "As a

parent, all you want is for your child to be safe. I hoped and fucking prayed to a God that abandoned me years ago that my son would be a geek and want to build planes or something but no, you had to go and be just like me." We both chuckle at that. "You wanting to lead isn't a bad thing, it's just hard for me to hand this all over to you when the time is right. The moment you become Don, Royal, there will always be a target on your back and I don't know how the fuck to live with that and find a way to be okay with it."

Suddenly, all the years of him telling me no to taking over and not giving a reason why makes sense. It was never because he was selfish or wanted to live forever and remain Don, it was because he didn't want to see someone come for me. Guilt gnaws away at my insides. I was a right cunt to my dad when all he was trying to do was protect me. I decide to listen to him for the first time in years and not fight him on this, he's under enough pressure and doesn't need me adding to it. I can't promise I won't still fuck with him and freeze his accounts or some shit like that, though.

"Havoc, Chaos, Sin and I will be on the first flight back to UNLV. I'll make sure we all stick together and stay out of trouble until you deal with this situation." Surprise has his eyes widening.

"Am I being Punk'd?" I frown.

"What's Punk'd?" He rolls his eyes and shakes his head.

"You were still swimming in my left sack when that show was around." My face contorts in disgust.

"That's fucking disgusting, I'm going now," I say as I stand to my feet with his laughter following me out the door. Just as I cross the threshold, he calls out to me. I pop my head back into his office and say,

"Yeah?"

"I love you, Royal, never doubt that."

Nodding and feeling slightly weird about all this emotional shit I mutter, "I love you too, old man." He curses me out as I stroll into the kitchen laughing, knowing that I got the last laugh.

Chapter Eleven

THANK FUCK MIAMI IS DONE!

Being away from my girls for two weeks is pure fucking torture. I miss Clare so much and I hate that I missed Nytress and Unique's national competition, but I got to see the videos that Clare sent me. I look down at the screensaver on my phone and smile, it's a picture of me and my three girls last Thanksgiving. Just the sight of the three of them has my heart expanding in my chest. I never thought I would ever make it to the age I am now, being thirty-nine and married with two beautiful daughters isn't something I ever saw in my future. Am I fucking glad life didn't go as I had envisioned it? Fuck, yes, I am!

"Fuck!" Bishop snaps from his seat across from me and scrubs a hand down his face, he looks frustrated and tired. This deal in Miami was a huge one, with Tony passing last year he left everything to Royal. My nephew has no idea that he will become the sole heir to his grandfather's fortune and all that entails when he turns twenty-one next year. Bishop and Kiara have chosen to keep that bit of information from their ambitious son, knowing he would drop out of college and move to Miami now. Bish and Royal clash a lot because he is so much like his father, headstrong and won't listen to anything anyone has to say.

"What happened?" Gage asks from his seat across the aisle from us. Vin sits next to him with a puzzled look on his face. King shifts next to Bishop to try to peer over his shoulder and look at his laptop. Knight snorts next to me causing me to smile. Knight and I both know that King has been taking on more of a leadership role in New York since Bish's time has been split between there and Miami.

"Fucking Royal!" Bish grits out through clenched teeth. It takes the five of us all of two seconds before we burst out laughing. Bishop shoots each of a glare, at the great joy it gives the five of us, knowing our nephew can ruffle his father's feathers. "It's not fucking funny!" he shouts.

"What'd he do?" Vin asks, even though he can't mask the humor in his voice.

"He fucking froze my accounts for the hotels in Miami and just donated a hundred fucking grand to some scholarship program!" We all lose it again. I'm laughing so hard, tears leak from the corner of my eyes. Bishop is muttering about us being dicks as he pulls his phone out and dials a number before bringing it to his ear—no doubt he's calling Kiara. We all sit and listen shamelessly to his conversation. King being the lifesaver, snatches Bish's phone and puts it on loudspeaker.

"Hey, babe," Kiara answers. Bish keeps his glare on King as he answers his wife.

"Your son is out of fucking control!" he snaps. Kiara sighs before asking what he did this time. Bish relays what he just told us.

"Babe, he donated to charity, how can you be mad at that?" Bish grinds his teeth so hard I fear he'll break them.

"He fucking froze my accounts, Kiara! The little shit spent too much fucking time with his stupid ass uncles and Koby." Royal learned to hack from Knight, Vin and Koby, and Bishop hates it. "He needs to be taught a lesson——." We all shake our heads and wave our hands trying to stop him but it's too late. The five of us shake our heads and slump back in our seats,

"Dumbass," Knight mutters.

"You want to teach my baby a lesson, huh?" Bishop's face pales as he realizes what he just said. If anyone ever says a single thing about Royal, his mother is there throwing hands in defense of her son.

"Baby, I didn't——" The princess cuts Bishop off.

"You touch a single fucking hair on my baby's head——"

"He's not a baby, he's twenty!" Bishop defends.

"Fucking try me, Bishop, you try to punish him or threaten to take away his birthright again and I will chop your fucking dick off!" Bish smiles and shakes his head.

"You're fucking perfect," he says in a tone that has me scrunching my face up in disgust.

"Don't try to butter me up." Eww, Kiara sounds fucking breathy.

"Is it working?" Before she can answer a loud boom sounds from the left side of the plane, alarms blare as the plane dips to the left and we are thrown about the cabin.

"The plane is on fire!" Vincent shouts. I peer out the window on his side as I grip the armrest of my chair, smoke is billowing out of the wing. Before anyone else can say a word another boom sounds out but from the right. The plane takes a nosedive and sends me sailing forward toward the cockpit door, I'm too slow to put my arms to break the fall and smack my head. Everything goes black.

I groan, blinking my eyes open as pain radiates throughout my whole body. I sit up and push pieces of debris off me. When I lift the food trolley off my leg I cry out in pain. Fuck! A bone sticks out of the side of my leg. I can't fucking move so I dart my gaze around the wreckage to try spot my brothers, but can't see them.

"Bishop?" I yell. "Knight, King, Gage, Vincent? Where the fuck are you?" I keep shouting their names for what feels like hours but is mere minutes until I hear someone call back.

"Rook?" Relief rushes through me at the sound of my twin's voice.

"Knight, I'm over here!" I almost fucking cry at the sight of him walking around the plane's tail, well limping. His shirt is torn and he looks fucking banged up but at least he's able to stand.

"Knight, Rook?" I sag at the sound of King's voice.

"Over here!" I call back, and when I see him and Vin walking toward us from the trees in the marshlands I sigh. King has his arm wrapped around Vin as he helps him to walk toward me. We all share a look as we stand—well, I sit. "Where's Bishop?" I ask hesitantly.

"Right fucking here!" I snap my head and look over my shoulder to see my brother limping toward us, his face littered with cuts, his suit torn and his arm looks hurt but he's alive and that's all that matters. He pats me on the shoulder as he gives King, Vin and Knight a hug. "Where the fuck is Gage?" he asks. I shake my head. He curses before he and Knight help me to my feet, I grit my teeth through the pain as we slowly hop along and make our way around the other side of the plane. Everything inside me stills at the sight of my brother on his knees clutching his stomach as blood pours from his wound.

"Gage!" I shout. His pale face lifts to me and the look of fear in his eyes has a lump forming in my throat. Men in suits surround him with guns trained on us and him. Bishop pushes me into Knight as he steps forward and morphs from worried brother to the Don of the Murdoch fucking mafia.

"Do you have any idea who you just fucking shot?" His tone is cold and devoid of all emotion but I can tell from how taut his muscles are that he is worried as fuck. We are all injured and have no weapons, we're sitting fucking ducks here. A guy with short-cropped hair and pale as fuck blue eyes step forward, buttoning his jacket. The dude looks so familiar but I can't place where I know him from.

"I know exactly who I shot. By the looks of things your brother doesn't have long before his lungs fill with blood and he drowns in it." Bish growls and steps forward, only pausing when the sound of guns cocking halts him.

"You're going to die for this," Bishop snarls, then turns to look at our brother who is turning white as a sheet. "On my honor, you will not fucking die. I won't allow it, do you hear me?" Bish's words seem to spark some life into Gage, he nods and tries to hide his pain.

"He and all of you will die. Then your son will sign over what was rightfully mine." At the mention of Royal,

Bishop stands taller and the tension bleeds out of his body. He and his son may fight, but Bishop would start World War III for his son in a heartbeat. No one fucks with his kid and lives to talk about it. "My name is Chance Bennett, and I am the only living relative of your wife and son."

Fuck, that's when it hits me.

"You're the governor of Florida?" He smiles brightly and nods.

"I am. Now, if you want your son and wife to remain breathing, you'll do as I say."

"What the fuck do you want?" Knight snarls.

"The six of you are getting on the next plane to Siberia. While I deal with my precious little cousin." I stiffen, anyone who gets sent to Siberia never comes back. It's a place worse than any prison, that place makes living with Tony Murdoch seem like a vacation. A dark chuckle escapes Bishop, the sound of it has Knight tensing beside me.

"Ship us away, do whatever you want but just know this... You may think my son is weak and uneducated in this life but I warn you now, Royal is worse than I ever was. He was trained by the best to hack, hunt and play the long game. Unlike me, my son isn't ruled by emotions so be ready because you will never see him coming until it's too late."

Chapter Twelve

Bishop

THE SIX OF US ARE LOADED INTO THE BACKS OF THEIR SUV's. I fight against these cunts to get to Gage as he's slumped in two of the bastards' holds. Vin rushes one of the guards and manages to get to Gage but before he can do more, a shot rings out. My eyes widen in horror as he crashes to the ground. I thrash in the cunts hold and manage to shake one of them off but the other pushes the barrel of his gun into the back of my head.

"Vincent?" I roar. Four guys in suits rush over and grab each of his arms and legs and carry him over to the same car as Gage. I have no idea if he is alive or not. I watch as their car drives off. Knight and Rook are shoved into another car that follows behind Vin and Gage's, King and I are placed in the same car as Chance. Two guards sit behind us with their guns pressed firmly into the backs of our heads. Chance rides shotgun as one of his bitch boys drives and follows behind the other two cars.

I spy King clutching his side out of the corner of my eyes, each of us are fucked up in some way from the crash. My heart is beating erratically, if anything happens to Vincent or Gage, I am going to lose my fucking mind and kill every single one of these cunts, governor or not, he will die slowly and painfully for what he has done. I try to wrack my brain for Anthony ever mentioning Kiara having a cousin. The old man told me who took out her mother's side of the family, so why would he never mention a nephew from his own side?

"You should have stayed in New York. All of this could have been avoided if you just stayed on your side but no, your greed knows no bounds." I grit my teeth through the pain in my ribs as the car jolts from hitting a bump on the dirt road.

"And you should have stayed in your mother's cunt but here we are." I laugh at King's comment while Chance peers over the side of his seat and nods. In the next second, King is pistol whipped on the back of the head and grunting in pain. I lean toward him only for the bastard to cock the trigger on his gun and point it at my brother.

"Make another move and you lose another brother."

Gritting my teeth, I slowly right myself in my chair and meet Chance's fucking gaze. The cunt smiles and the rage that simmers inside me reaches new heights.

"I am going to kill you," I grit out.

"Pretty hard to kill someone when you are outmanned and outgunned, isn't it?" I quirk a condescending brow.

"Who said I needed a gun to kill your bitch ass?"

His eyes narrow and his upper lip twitches. I can tell already he is no henchman, he is the pussy that sits behind a desk and sends someone else to do his dirty work. There is no way this fucker has ever taken a life before, he's too clean-cut and way too fucking cocky to have ever seen someone die in front of him.

"They said you were a mouthy bastard." I fight to keep the confusion off my face, but from the way his eyes light up and he smiles wide enough to show teeth, I know I must have failed. "Oh, did you really think your little peace meeting went well, did you?"

Now it all clicks. He knew we were in Miami because it was a setup, the whole fucking thing was a trap and I flew my family right into it.

"You're working with the Vargas cartel." It isn't a question, it's a statement. King groans beside me and some of the tension eases from me knowing that he is okay.

"You killed their heir, what did you expect to happen? They were never going to forgive that indiscretion. They are the fucking cartel, they don't do forgiveness."

I thought it was too easy, which is why I had a contingency plan put in place just in case of an ambush. I just hope my son is as smart as I give him credit for and finds it.

"Where are you taking us?" King grits out through clenched teeth. Chance ignores his question and turns around in his seat, dismissing us. King looks at me and I can tell without him saying a single word, he's worried.

I make sure to keep the worry I feel inside me off my face. He needs me to be strong and reassure him that we are making it out of this fucked-up situation alive. The fear and worry I feel isn't for myself, it's for my brothers. Vincent isn't just my brother-in-law, I class him as one of my brothers and losing him would hurt me the same as losing one of the others. My main focus right now is getting to Gage and making sure he is okay. I know he needs medical attention and if he doesn't get it fast, he's going to die.

We pull up to a private airfield, security man the gates. I discreetly peer through the gap in the front seats to see there are eight more blacked out SUVs parked in a half circle near where a cargo plane sits. The moment we roll through the gates, the doors on the other SUVs open and men begin to pile out. I stiffen in my seat at the sight of Emelio Vargas, the head of the Vargas cartel. I watch as the fuckers that nabbed us from the crash site drag my four brothers out into the center of the bastards and force them to their knees. Gage slumps forward and Knight quickly reaches out to grab him before he can face plant on the ground. His eyes are closed. Worry churns inside me at the sight of him so deathly pale. Vincent's shirt is soaked with blood from the gunshot wound.

The moment our car stops, guards rush forward and yank mine and King's doors open and haul us out of the car. Each of my arms are restrained by the two fuckers who drag me toward my brothers—that's the only reason I don't fight, because I need to get closer to them to make sure Gage is actually breathing.

I grunt when they force me to my knees on the opposite side of the others and my teeth clash together from the force. I run my gaze over Gage and sigh when I see his chest rising and falling.

"How the mighty have fallen." I flick my gaze to Emelio and make sure he can see the unfiltered hatred in my gaze. I was a fool for thinking there was a peaceful way to end this. I will never make that same mistake twice.

"What the fuck do you want?" I grit out. His eyes narrow before he gives the fucker behind me a curt nod. I know what's coming so I brace for impact but it does nothing to diminish the pain that explodes in the back of my head. I slump forward and grunt in pain.

"You motherfucker!"

"I'll kill you!" Rook and King shout. I'm hauled back to my knees by the collar of my shirt, I shoot a look to my brothers and give them a subtle shake of my head to remain silent and let me deal with this.

"Let them go and you can have me," I say. The moment the twins, King and even Vincent manage to protest, I shoot them all a look that has them clamping their mouths shut. I may be their brother but now isn't the time for that shit to come into play, at this moment I am their Don and that's all.

"No," Chance grits out as he comes to stand beside Emelio. "You will all remain together until I am assured that your son and my cousin can adhere to my demands and hand over all your operations to the Vargas cartel. I fight to keep the shock off my face, that's what this is about? Chance promised Emelio he could have my territories if they helped him take us down so he could get his revenge against his uncle for abandoning him.

"At least get my brother some fucking medical help," Knight snaps. Emelio opens his mouth to say something but then a young blonde woman in a suit hops out of the back of his vehicle and stands directly in front of him. Her hands moving a mile a minute but no words escape her, that's when I realize she's deaf.

"Fine, fine, now get the hell back in the car," he snaps

at the young woman. Is that his daughter? Before she climbs into the back of the car she looks to me and smiles crookedly, her hazel eyes shine with delight. She does something with her hands but I don't know sign language so I make sure to store those movements in the back of mind to look up when I get the fuck out of here. "Get on that plane and don't make a scene and I'll call a helicopter here within minutes to take your brother and brother-in-law to a hospital to get the best medical attention money can buy."

I don't hesitate. "Deal." Emelio turns to the side and nods to one of his goonies who stalks off and makes a call.

"Where the fuck are you sending us?" Rook snaps.

Chance smiles and rubs his hands together. "Siberia is beautiful this time of year." Rook fails at keeping the fear off his face.

"Get them the help they need and we will cause no problems," I growl.

"You don't have the advantage here to make demands," Chance grits out. I don't bother to look at him. I answer, keeping my gaze fixed on Emelio.

"You made a grave mistake siding with him. I was prepared to bury this conflict between us but not now."

The fucker snarls. "I know you didn't kill my son but I do know that your fucking children had something to do with it. Make no mistake, I'm coming for them next." My brothers begin to shout out their protests.

"Quiet." At the booming sound of my voice the four

of them shut the fuck up. I smile up at Chance and Emelio as the sound of helicopter blades can be heard in the distance. Thank fuck, Gage is going to make it. "Send your best men after them, as many as you have." They both frown. "My son, the twins and my niece are the best at what they do. You won't know they have you where they want you until it's too late. They are the Memento Mori and they will remind you that death isn't optional."

They say nothing as the helicopter lands and paramedics rush over with a stretcher to load Gage on it. I pray to a God who turned his back on me years ago to not take my brother from me. Vincent is helped to his feet, supported by a paramedic and led toward the helicopter. On his way past he winks down at me, it was so fast I wouldn't have seen it if I wasn't paying such close attention to him. My eyes are drawn to his hands that are cuffed behind his back and that's when I see it, his wedding band is no longer gold, it's black.

I nod my understanding. Vincent is always one step ahead and because of that, he was smart enough to switch out his wedding ring before we left New York and replaced it with one that is fitted with a tracker so my sister and the others will be able to track him and Gage.

"Get their asses on the plane," Chance orders. Guards haul the four of us to our feet, but before we can be led to the plane Emelio steps in front of me, his dark eyes boring into mine.

"Killing your heir is going to be the sweetest revenge."

I lurch forward and manage to headbutt the cunt and relish the groan of pain that tears from him, then I'm yanked backward before I can do it again.

"Touch my son and I'll fucking kill you!" I roar. The cunt just smiles.

"Once I deal with your son, I may even take your wife to bed just so she knows what it's like to be fucked by a real man before I put a bullet between her eyes." I'm dragged toward the plane screaming out threats and cursing each of those cunts. I will never stop fighting to get back to my family. I will do whatever the fuck I need to do to make sure my wife and son survive this war even if it means the end of my life.

Now is the time for you to take over, my son, be the leader I know you can be and protect our family until I can get back. It's time for you to Reign Royal.

Want to know what happens next?
Find in book 1 of the Memento Mori series,
Reign Of Royal..
https://mybook.to/ReignOfRoyal

THANK YOU!

I am so thankful to have been able to come back and dive back into the OG's as well as give you all a taste of the next gen of Murdochs. I know you are mad about that *tiny* cliffhanger but don't fret, all will be explained in Royal's book coming next month. *Reign of Royal* will be the start of the next generation.

I can't thank you enough for loving each of the OG's the way I do and taking a chance on the next gen, their series is out of this world and so much more fucked up than their parents!

Keep an eye out for the Memento Mori series.

If you loved Stalemate, I would appreciate it if you could please leave a review on Amazon, Bookbub or Goodreads.

Paranormal Romance

The Dream Series

A Beautiful Dream

A Twisted Fate

A Beautiful Nightmare

Redemption

Anarchy

Brutal Savages

Savage Lies

Brutal Truth

Savage Beast

Brutal Beauty

Mafia Romance

Murdoch Mafia Series

Played By The Bishop

Tormented By The King

Tortured By The Knight

Tempted By The Queen

Turned By The Pawn

Ruined By The Rook

Murdoch Mafia Novella

Stalemate

Memento Mori Series

Reign Of Royal

Broken By Sin

In Havoc Lays Chaos

Fairytales With A Twist

Condemned Beast

Sports Romance

Playing For Keeps

Offside

Touchdown

End Game

Hail Mary

Blindside

RH Sports

Hate Us Like You Mean It

Love Me Like You Mean It

ACKNOWLEDGMENTS

Marcus, you have been a fucking G while I wrote this book and I appreciate you so much for all the NSFW's you have drawn for this series, on the real though you don't pay me enough to be your PA.

My devils in disguise, you two are my reason for existing, my inspiration, my muses, my whole fucking world. Without the two of you I am nothing, you bring so much joy and laughter to mine and your fathers lives, thank you for choosing me to be your mum.

My proofreader, Sarah, thank you so much for always making these books what they are and never hiding your thoughts of the flow or consistency's in the stories from me. Your honesty is the reason why these books are what they are, could not have asked for a more amazing proofer. I fucking love you and cherish you babe.

Clare Bear, you have transitioned from alpha girl to developmental editor and I couldn't be more honoured to have had you work on this book, thank you so much for taking a chance on me and allowing me to be your first client. Love you!

My Beta girls, Debbie, Carla, Chanel, Morgan and Nicole. Thank you ladies so much for jumping on this doc and working your magic! You badass's are the real MVPS.

My Army: Alicia, Amber, Angel, Ash, Barb, Charlotte, Cyndi, Christina, Jasmine, Jen, Kahanna, Katelyn, Kylie, Lakshmi, Lora, Lyndsey, Rebecca, Rizzo, Sarmi, Sonya, Terri and Tess. Thank you ladies so fucking much for being the best freaking team an author could ask for. Without all of you I wouldn't be here and your support and constant love of each of these characters means more than you will ever know xxx

My street team, thank you so much for everything you do and all the shares as well as pimping out each of these books all over the socials. You ladies are amazing! Thank you for sticking by me and loving each of these men and women the way you do.

My editor, Lizz, you are the bomb.com and no one can tell me otherwise. Thank you for always fitting me in and helping me perfect these books. None of these would be what they are without you, thank you my friend.

Leah Maree, what more can I say aside from I bow down to you Guru. You are the most fantastic human I have ever met. You, my dark little soul, are amazing and I fucking love you. Thank you for all the teasers and these amazing as fuck covers. I couldn't do any of this without ya, babe.

Last but not least, you, my amazing readers, mean everything to me! Without you none of this would be possible. Thank you for your continued support and reading my books. It still stuns me to get messages from you telling me you love my books. I really am living my dream and that's thanks to you.

Sam Xxx

One day I will get a mention in the books for being such an amazing friend and formatting your books for free. I'm confident I have paid off my NSFW by now since I wouldn't blow your husband for payment.

-The one and only famous JAYE PRATT.

P.S - I was also nice enough to put your name on my books because I'm so famous I can do that.

ABOUT THE AUTHOR

Samantha Barrett is a dark romance, PNR author who loves to write out-of-the-box stories. She is originally from the land of the long white cloud, New Zealand. She is totally fluking her way through this whole author gig, if she isn't writing you can find her kicking back with her kids and husband with a bag of chips and a glass of wine in her hand.

Sam loves Twilight and is a TWIHARD proudly.